Graziella

Graziella

/ A Novel /

Alphonse de Lamartine

Translated and with an Introduction by
Raymond N. MacKenzie

University of Minnesota Press
Minneapolis
London

The University of Minnesota Press gratefully acknowledges
the generous assistance provided for the publication of this book
by the College of Arts and Sciences at the University
of St. Thomas.

Published by the University of Minnesota Press
111 Third Avenue South, Suite 290
Minneapolis, MN 55401-2520
http://www.upress.umn.edu

Printed in the United States of America on acid-free paper

The University of Minnesota is an equal-opportunity educator
and employer.

24 23 22 21 20 19 18   10 9 8 7 6 5 4 3 2 1

Library of Congress Cataloging-in-Publication Data
Names: Lamartine, Alphonse de, 1790–1869 author. | MacKenzie,
    Raymond N. translator.
Title: Graziella / Alphonse de Lamartine ; translated and with an
    introduction by Raymond N. MacKenzie.
Other titles: Graziella. English
Description: Minneapolis : University of Minnesota Press, 2018. |
Identifiers: LCCN 2018001922 (print)| ISBN 978-1-5179-0247-6 (hc)
    ISBN 978-1-5179-0248-3 (pb)
Classification: LCC PQ2325.G6 E5 2018 (print) | DDC 843/.7–dc23
LC record available at https://lccn.loc.gov/2018001922

CONTENTS

TRANSLATOR'S INTRODUCTION

Raymond N. MacKenzie

Lamartine's *Graziella* enjoyed an enormous readership and an almost universal acclamation throughout the nineteenth century. There were skeptics and naysayers even when the book was new—Flaubert the foremost among them—but the story captured the imagination of a vast number of readers across Europe and America.[1] And it is by no means forgotten even today: one can take Graziella tours on the islands of Procida and Ischia, visiting what purports to be her house (though Lamartine tells us it was long gone even during his lifetime), and even observing Procida's annual summertime Miss Graziella beauty contest. The book has its faults: there is some histrionic dialogue, and some aspects of the denouement may not sit well with a modern, realist-minded reader. But it is nonetheless a fascinating tale with many beautiful moments, an evocative, mythic air, and much that is ripe for analysis with regard to its views on love, on social class, on men and women.

The book gains in richness, too, the more one knows about its context, its composition, and its author. To begin with the essential contradiction: *Graziella* is presented to us as memoir, as fact, but it is a work of fiction in nearly every detail as well as in its larger plot. And even more strangely, Lamartine seems to have believed in the story, insisting on its truth over and over in the course of his life-time with an intensity that makes the book ever more in-triguing. We are drawn into its dizzying *âbime* of truth and fiction, of "higher truths" and invention, of the memory of what was and the desire for what might have been—or should have been. The ghostly presence of the palimpsest that is Graziella begins to haunt us, just as she haunted Lamartine.

The story of Graziella takes place over the winter and spring of 1811–12. Lamartine and his young French friend (unnamed, but clearly his close friend from his school years, Aymon de Virieu) are on their own in a foreign country for the first time. Both are from the privileged classes, minor aristocrats in fact. Both have the aristocratic *particule* "de" prefixing their family names, but Lamartine's family has little money to go with it, whereas Virieu's family is very well off. Like tourists trying out different modes of living, they befriend an old fisherman outside Naples and talk him into taking them on as helpers. The life is ex-otic, freeing, and it serves as a kind of short-term rebellion (or as we might term it today, a "gap year") before settling down and returning to take up the social and political du-ties that await them back in France. Through Virieu's fi-nancial generosity, they buy a boat to replace one wrecked in a tempest, and before long the two are living with the family on the islands in the Bay of Naples. The family includes the beautiful young girl Graziella, and friendship with her turns to sisterly/brotherly affection. Eventually Graziella falls deeply in love with Lamartine. He is unsure what to make of it, and although he recognizes and re-spects the depth of her feelings, he does not really return them. Her love grows more desperate, and after a number of incidents—one of which involves Graziella's belief in the Madonna's miraculous powers—Lamartine is called home. He promises to return, but she wastes away, seeming to know they will never again be together, and she dies before the end of the year. Her memory becomes a lasting sorrow to Lamartine. Such is the story, presented to us in the first person, as a memoir.

Lamartine: Poetry and Politics

Lamartine (1790–1869) has never been known as a novelist; on the contrary, he was one of the greatest Romantic poets of his century, second only perhaps to Victor Hugo. In 1820 (eight years after the Graziella episode), at the age of thirty, he published his first collection of poems, *Méditations poétiques*, and it took the reading world by storm. No French poet had written with such frank self-revelation together with such easy mastery of technique, such fluency; the poems were personal, emotional, passionate, and readers responded, at first in the royalist salons, and then among the wider public: the book went through nine editions in the first two years.

Lamartine went on to numerous other literary successes and a great deal more poetry, but what he most wanted was a political career. Poetry, master of it though he was, would only be of use if it led him into the political arena. Like Lord Byron, whom he resembles in a number of ways, he had a messianic strain in his character; like Byron, he was deeply immersed in politics; and like Byron, women found him irresistible—so much so that trying to untangle the truth about his various and very numerous love affairs is, as we shall see, not easy. But success in love, like success in poetry, did not immediately translate into success in politics: in the years before *Méditations*, he had been struggling from one low-level diplomatic post to another, always seeking a position of some significance or impact, and never finding his footing despite the connections his aristocratic background and family gave him. To understand some of the complex contexts of *Graziella*, we need to begin with Lamartine's political career and slowly work backward to the events that the novel narrates. This is a roundabout approach, but *Graziella* is a work consisting of layers of memory and fiction, and it is best appreciated when the reader, like Lamartine, approaches the story from a multilayered retrospective. A chronology is included on pages 137–38 of this text; the reader may wish to refer to it from time to time, as this introduction seeks to untangle the skein of names and events that underlie the novel.

In the 1830s and '40s, while he continued to write prolifically, Lamartine's primary energies increasingly went into politics, as an elected member of the *Chambre des Députés*. Over those decades, his views slowly evolved from an early royalism to a progressive republicanism. He stayed aloof from the major parties, insisting on his independence, and he became practiced in spreading his proto-socialist views beyond the Chambre. He had a deep-seated belief that he was destined for greatness and doing benefit to humankind, and while he became very good at what we more suspicious moderns might call self-promotion, this was never cynical on his part but, rather, seems to have stemmed from a genuine belief that he was a man of destiny, from a messianic sense of himself. He saw himself as a man in the mold of Chateaubriand or even Voltaire, as Roger Pearson puts it, "never wavering in his self-assessment as an indispensable leader of mankind."[2] In *Graziella*, among so much that is fictional, this description of himself and his friend Virieu rings true:

> There could have been no role, no matter how heroic,
> that we would not have risen to, given the situation.

> We were prepared for anything, and if fate failed to
> present us with the grand circumstances we imagined,
> we would avenge ourselves by our contempt for fate.
> We felt the consolation that strong hearts always feel:
> that if our lives ended up unimportant, vulgar, and
> obscure, it was destiny that had failed us, and not we
> that failed destiny!

This idealism was not confined to his youthful years; it continued to motivate the adult Lamartine, the deputé, and later, minister of state.

In 1843, he founded his own newspaper, *Le Bien public* (the public good), and in 1847, he published an enormously influential history of the French Revolution, titled *Histoire des Girondins*. The book advocated the idea that the Revolution need not have devolved into the Terror, that the chaos and carnage of the early 1790s had been by no means inevitable. The *Girondins* book blended solid historical research with his own opinions—progressive not radical opinions, and rational not wild-eyed or prophetic views on social progress. In fact, the year 1847 saw two other books reinterpreting the French Revolution; the others, though they were written by the important historians Louis Blanc and Jules Michelet, had a small readership compared to the enormous sales and impact that Lamartine's had.[3] Everyone was reading the book, and the idea that a new revolution need not be a catastrophe began to take root among the wider public, along with the idea that indeed it might actually make an improvement on the restored monarchy, which had been growing more and more unpopular. The *Girondins*, says William Fortescue, "came to be widely regarded as one of the causes of the February 1848 Revolution."[4] And when revolution did break out, Lamartine was one of the five leaders who guided the fledgling government; indeed, for a time he was the de facto leader of the country. Richard Sennett paints a vivid picture of Lamartine's influence by following him on a single, critical day, February 24, when mobs were forming and the revolution was in danger of slipping into anarchy. Sennett shows him going out to speak to the crowds seven different times on that day alone, each time calming them and saving the day by the sheer charisma of his character:

> He does not plead with the mob or seek to mollify
> them. He challenges them instead. He recites poetry,
> he tells them he knows what it is to be alive at a revo-
> lutionary moment. He calls them fools, he tells them
> flatly that they do not understand what is happening.
> He is not condescending; he is outraged by them and
> lets them know it.[5]

For Sennett, Lamartine that spring of 1848 was one of the great examples of the power of sheer personality in politics.

Those spring months were to be the apex of Lamartine's political career. He was not an extreme leftist (though he was friendly with the far left), but he was one of the chief moving forces behind abolishing slavery in the colonies, establishing universal male suffrage, and outlawing the death penalty for political crimes (thus ensuring that 1848 would not go the way that the 1790s did); he also was instrumental in the movement toward universal free education. His popularity across all levels of French society was extraordinary; the press referred to him affectionately as "the poet," and it was generally assumed for a time that he would be the first president of the new republic. But when that universal suffrage was finally implemented and the election was held in December 10, Lamartine came in fourth among the major candidates, and a weak fourth at that. Louis-Napoléon Bonaparte won in a landslide, with more than five million votes; Lamartine would garner just under eighteen thousand.[6] As Sennett puts it: "After mid-May the people of the streets quickly tired of Lamartine. They became indifferent, as though they had exchanged their own willingness to be dominated for his person; by May's end, they had squeezed him dry."[7] Between the glorious days of February and the election of December, the country shifted to the right, and Lamartine was never again as powerful a voice as he had been in the spring. Worse, his beloved republic would be undone by Louis-Napoléon only two years later, when the Empire was declared. Thus ended a lifetime of political ambition.

Elvire / Graziella / Julie / Antoniella

But there was no lapse in his celebrity, which reached new heights with the publication of an autobiographical work—serialized in *La Presse* beginning on January 2, 1849, immediately on the heels of the election—titled *Les Confidences*. Its English translation was rushed into print the same year for an eager readership in America and given the title *Confidential Disclosures*.[8] And it is within this volume that readers first encountered the tale of the fisherman's family and the beautiful teenage girl Graziella. In *Confidences*, the tale is simply titled "Graziella: Episode," and it comes between chapters VI and IX. But that "episode" stood out so brilliantly and was so much read and discussed that in 1852, Lamartine published it by itself in book form as *Graziella*.

As far back as the 1820 volume of poems, *Méditations*, Lamartine was writing about a mysterious beloved woman; he called her Elvire then, and she figured in four of the poems of the collection.[9] The poems revealed few concrete facts except for the essentials: their love had been powerful, all-consuming, and she was now deceased. In death, Elvire took on the role of muse, as if her death had unleashed the poet within the lover. Her death, her absence: these seem to be essential. Deborah Jenson analyzes what she calls Lamartine's "rhetoric born of pain" in his early poems, and she concludes that he uses that rhetoric for a single, focusing purpose: "To give voice, make present, resuscitate, and unify what is silenced, lost, dead, fragmented. The genre of this glorified poetic agency is the elegy; its object, the feminine muse."[10] Pain, and especially the pain of loss, makes the poet. We see this process replicated in the text of *Graziella*, where in a coda the sight of a young girl's funeral inspires the poem "Le Premier Regret."

The dead beloved woman as inspiring object: literature and paintings of the European nineteenth century are teeming with it, from the vampiric woman of Gautier's *La Morte amoureuse*, to the poisonous daughter of Rappaccini in Hawthorne, to the Madeline Usher of Poe, the literature of the era seems fascinated with the association of the beloved female and death. Elisabeth Bronfen's study of the phenomenon notes one particularly important aspect of this: "[The] image of a feminine corpse presents a concept of beauty which places the work of death into the service of the aesthetic process, for this form of beauty is contingent on the translation of an animate body into a deanimated one. Beauty fascinates not only because it is unnatural, but also because it is precarious."[11] This seems precisely to describe the situation Lamartine presents in the coda sequence. The body in the coffin somehow gives birth to the poem. Or as Bronfen puts it, "the feminine corpse inspires the surviving man to write."[12]

Moreover, Lamartine sees the funeral when he is

standing inside a church, and this is no coincidence, for religious diction and imagery proliferate and surround the absent figure of Elvire: his love for her is a *"feu sacré,"* a holy fire. As Paul Viallaneix puts it: "Lamartine introduced something new into Romantic religion, a religion that always refused to be limited only to the teachings of revelation: a new hope, through the figure of the mediating woman, and a new dogma of redemptive love."[13] Elvire might have been a poetic fiction, a figure in the tradition of Dante's Beatrice, Petrarch's Laura, or more recently, Eléonore, the idealized muse of the recently deceased poet Évariste-Désiré de Forges, Vicomte de Parny. But in 1820, any reader in the know would have naturally assumed that Elvire was simply a coded version of Madame Julie Charles, who had died in 1817. The story of Lamartine and Julie Charles was an open secret.

Julie Charles, née Julie Bouchaud des Hérettes, was born in 1784 in Santo Domingo, the mixed-race daughter of a plantation owner. She married Jacques Charles (1746–1823), a celebrated physician and scientist, inventor of the altimeter, and the first man to fly in a hydrogen balloon. His beautiful young Creole wife became known as one of the premier salon hostesses in Paris, gathering together eminent thinkers, writers, and scientists; she was a fiery royalist, her family having been ruined during the Revolution, and she had all the wit and powers of expression that establishing and maintaining such a salon required. But she was inclined to maladies of the lungs, and in October 1816 her husband sent her to the spa town of Aix-les-Bains to recover, or at least to slow the progress of her tuberculosis. There she stayed in the Hotel Chabert, a pension near Lac du Bourget. At that same time, the young Alphonse de Lamartine—twenty-six, underemployed, and suffering from various vague ailments—came to Aix for a rest cure and happened to lodge at the same place. The two met in the most romantic of circumstances: she was boating on the lake when a storm came up, her boat was foundering, and her life was in danger. She fainted away, and Lamartine, watching from his own boat, rowed toward hers and eventually got her ashore, unconscious. She awoke to find the tall, handsome young man gazing earnestly down at her. Not surprisingly, a passionate love flared up quickly between the two.

When she returned to Paris, their love only intensified, but her health continued to decline and the opportunities to be alone together were fewer and fewer. In August 1817, Lamartine returned to Aix-les-Bains where the two had planned to meet again, but this time she was too sick to travel. Lamartine stayed on without her, and in September he wrote what has become his single most famous poem, and one of the greatest of French Romantic lyrics, "Le Lac." The theme of the poem is, like so many Romantic works, how our feelings interact with our external realities, and in the present time of the poem, the poet is alone, contemplating the memory of the absent beloved; "Le Lac" dramatizes an evening the two had spent together the year before, with the unnamed beloved woman entreating time to slow its flight.

As we have seen, Lamartine had been writing a number of poems with the theme of an absent beloved, and he sent them with some trepidation to Julie Charles during their months apart just before Christmas of 1816; he delegated his good friend Aymon de Virieu to bring her the poems and to read them to her. Virieu did as requested and did it well. Madame Charles was startled at the poems and their power, and there is no doubt that her enthusiasm would, over the next several months, get his poetic reputation off to a good start, well before he had actually published anything. Among the pieces delivered and read by Virieu were the Elvire poems. This Elvire was clearly not Julie Charles herself, but someone else, someone he must have loved before her. Far from being jealous, though, she was moved, and in one letter she exclaimed, "Oh, my Alphonse! Who could ever bring Elvire back to you? And who was ever loved as she was? And who could deserve to be loved like that?"[14]

Lamartine had instructed Virieu not to reveal who Elvire actually was, because of the class distinction: he knew that Julie Charles could not accept his having been the lover of a lower-caste girl. As Maurice Toesca puts it, Lamartine's lie was inevitable and would have been entirely understandable for people of the era: "Any liaison between a gentleman and a woman of the people would be dishonorable."[15] Whatever she suspected, Julie Charles seemed to have accepted the mystery. The letters that survive show that her passion for Lamartine never abated—indeed, she probably loved him far more intensely than he did her. He visited her salon in Paris when he could, though their long-planned reunion at Aix would not come to pass. She died December 18, 1817, in Paris. Lamartine published his first book, *Méditations*, in March 1820. Included were the Elvire poems as well as the newer "Le Lac" and other poems clearly about Julie Charles, among them the beautiful poem on the bereaved lover's isolation, "L'Isolement." A reader in 1820 who had heard any of the gossip about Lamartine and Madame Charles would have concluded that she was Elvire, and indeed that misidentification would linger for a long time. For example, when in 1905 the scholar René Doumic published her letters to Lamartine, he titled the collection *Lettres d'Elvire à Lamartine*. But Julie Charles was not Elvire. In the 1850 edition of Lamartine's collected works, he added a commentary in which he said that Elvire was in fact Graziella.[16]

But who was Graziella? This absent muse, the girl who died and then served as inspiration, was the Elvire of the early poems. But the story of Graziella was written in 1844, two decades after the events it depicts—that is, after Julie Charles, after Lena deLarch (another love affair, this time in 1819), and after Lamartine's marriage to the Englishwoman Mary Ann Birch (rechristened Marianne later) in 1820.[17] And it was after his ascent into national politics. He was also working on his *Histoire des Girondins* at this time, and he took his family and his usual traveling entourage on a working vacation to Naples and the islands that were so important in his memory, Ischia and Procida. Also accompanying him was his niece, the twenty-three-year-old Valentine de Cessiat, who adored her uncle and would for the rest of her life.[18] The attentions of a beautiful young girl in a setting so steeped in memories helped Lamartine in many ways as he set about writing what became *Graziella*, including reviving his youthful eroticism. His wife, Marianne, was often ill, and their marriage was stable but never passionate. After many years of sexual adventuring, he appears to have settled down into a consistent fidelity to Marianne. But the fundamental eroticism in his nature, and the erotic impulse in his art, had not deserted him.

Hence, Valentine's presence in 1844 is of great importance. Jean des Cognets, an insightful critic of Lamartine in the early twentieth century, argued that the whole tale of Graziella was probably conceived for Valentine and would not have come about without her. Indeed, even his love for Julie Charles would become transfigured under the influence of his adoring niece, according to des Cognets: "The spiritual and quasi-mystical feeling attributed to the Neapolitan girl and to the Creole [Julie Charles] existed nowhere apart from within the heart of Valentine. She is the only one who actually felt, and revealed to the poet, the true Lamartinian love, in which the body plays no part, and in which God is reflected in souls that are wholly pure."[19] While Abel Verdier, from the ensuing generation of Lamartine scholars, vigorously disputed this, insisting that Lamartine's central conception, this pure, semi-theological vision of love, had always been present in the poet's work, des Cognets's interpretation nonetheless remains a compelling way to account for the sudden flowering of imagination that began in 1844 and continued through the writing and publication of not only *Graziella* but also *Raphaël*.

For *Raphaël* also was conceived during that 1844 return journey to Ischia and Naples. *Raphaël*, published in January 1849, the same month that *Confidences* began to appear serially in *La Presse*, is a lightly fictionalized retelling of Lamartine's love affair with Julie Charles. It appeared as a novel, though, and not as a memoir, and ironically Lamartine sticks more closely to facts in the so-called novel *Raphaël* than he does in what appears to be the memoir, *Graziella*. *Raphaël*, however, never captured the wide public that *Graziella* did; it is, as we would say today, talky, often inert with lengthy debates on God and religion, culminating in a religious conversion that feels false. And its insistence on the chastity of the two lovers, which is credible and even moving in *Graziella*, feels more like an attempt to shore up the posthumous reputation of Julie Charles than a depiction of the way things really were. Nonetheless, the book has its grand moments, some of them in many of its authorial asides. When Raphaël/ Lamartine and the beloved are separated, they write long, formless, even ungrammatical letters to each other:

[Those letters] were my soul stripped bare, standing before the soul of an other, expressing or rather
stammering as best it could about the tumultuous
sensations roiling within it: this language was not
made to express the inexpressible; imperfect signs,
empty words, hollow words, language of ice, which
the plenitude, the concentration, and the fire of our
soul cause to reshape, like some refractory metal,
into I don't know what vague, ethereal, flamboyant,
caressing language, a language of flames that no one
other than ourselves could ever understand, because it
simply was ourselves![20]

There are many points of contact, not surprisingly,
between *Graziella* and *Raphaël*. Both look back over two
decades to an idyllic, even Edenic moment; the beloved
woman proves to be physically weaker than she appears
and ultimately dies, while her memory serves as a kind
of lifelong inspiration to the surviving male lover. Setting
in both is essential: in the one, the Bay of Naples, and in
the other, the Lac du Bourget, give birth to life-changing
emotion. And both stories have their origin, as stories, in
the 1844 return to Ischia in the presence of Valentine.

Memoir and Fiction

Thus, many works started life in the 1844 trip to Naples,
including various new poems and the idea for an autobi-
ography, to be titled *Confidences*. Lamartine was habituated
to living like a country gentleman, with three country es-
tates and a home in Paris, but he was perennially short of
money, and books were a good way of generating cash.
He was negotiating with two publishers, Gosselin and
Béthune, for a series of volumes to be ready between 1844
and 1849—the *Girondins*, poems, the memoir—for which

he would be paid ultimately 710,000 francs, a much-needed infusion of cash, which would help keep creditors temporarily at bay.[21] The preface to *Confidences* details how Lamartine would never have published such material if it were not necessary in order to raise the money to hold on to his beloved family estate in Milly. (Interestingly, while the threat to the estate was real, the plan to write and sell the book long predated the threat.) For Lamartine after his first book, *Méditations*, publishing was always a matter of generating income, and his negotiations with publishers were usually fully detailed in his letters, and sometimes, as in the preface to *Confidences*, within the published book itself.[22]

He began with drafting the tale of *Graziella*, a memoir of events that took place over the winter and spring of 1811–12. He tells us in that same preface that he was writing the tale within sight of the ruins of her house when he was interrupted by a visitor, Eugène Pelletan.[23] He let Pelletan read the pages he had completed and noted that his visitor seemed moved by them. Lamartine goes on to narrate how Pelletan returned to Paris, excited about the book that would be *Confidences*, and told a publisher about them. The publisher's offer, a very generous one, arrived just when Lamartine's financial troubles were at their peak.[24] All this detail about his financial need serves to underwrite a number of things: the authenticity of the stories the reader is about to encounter in the *Confidences* volume, Lamartine's motives in publishing a personal book like this, and, indirectly, Lamartine's own honesty and trustworthiness. Thus there is no reason to think that the events narrated in the Graziella section, which occupies Books VII–VIII of *Confidences*, are anything but confidential disclosures. And certainly that is how reading audiences took them.

In that Graziella sequence, we learn that the eighteen-year-old Lamartine was sent to Italy with some relatives to get him out of an embarrassing romantic entanglement with Henriette Pommier, daughter of the local justice of the peace. This was true, but with the interesting difference that Lamartine was actually twenty-one at the time. Shaving those few years off brings him closer in age to Graziella and perhaps casts a greater aura of innocence over the young romantic hero. He was, however, anything but chaste and innocent; indeed, Lamartine was quite sexually precocious, for even before the Henriette affair he had fathered his first child at age fifteen with a village girl. And there had been another love affair with a girl from a neighboring village, Caroline Pascal. Around the same time he had begun writing poetry, which alarmed his mother, a highly religious and sober person, almost as much as his sexual adventures; she worried that he was morbidly introspective and had the boy sent off to relatives in Lyon to get him away from bad influences. There he got into more trouble, for he now discovered the pleasures of gambling as well as those of prostitutes and got himself into serious debt.[25] He was brought home, at which point his mother burned his volume of Rousseau, seeking someone to blame for her brilliant but difficult son. Around this time Lamartine's friendship with his schoolfellow Aymon de Virieu began to grow stronger, and the two began corresponding when they could not be together in person. None of these pre-1811 realities, however, was to make it into the pages of *Graziella*.

A full listing of the differences between the tale as told in *Graziella* and what we know really happened, or between the real Lamartine and the Lamartine who figures in the book, would be a very long one. The dates are wrong, the narrator's age is off, the presence and/or absence of Virieu is inconsistent, and so on. Of course none of these would matter—artists have always used a meld of fact and fiction—if it weren't for the way Lamartine presents the story as factual, right in the middle of *Confidences*. Toward the end of his life, Lamartine returned to the same years of his youth that had been covered in *Confidences*, in the book that was posthumously titled *Mémoires inédits, 1790–1815*.[26] (The relevant sections of the *Mémoires* are translated in the Appendix.) Lamartine, writing in the late 1860s, assures us that now he is going to set the record straight. He explains how he arrived in Naples and came to visit his relative's cigar factory, where the sight of female workers was among the first things he records:

> Young girls were passing in and out of the doors
> constantly, carrying I don't know what in their aprons.
> I learned later that these were children charged with
> picking out the tobacco leaves for making cigarettes. I
> was far from the thought that one of these girls would
> before long become *Graziella*, change her occupa-
> tion, dominate my destiny, and exert an imperishable
> influence over my entire life. But that was true; we
> will see how it all came about. I did not dare tell the
> story when I wrote the true novel, *Graziella*, in 1847,[27]
> which had and still has such popularity, because all
> readers recognize the true accent of nature in it. I
> slightly altered some of the opening pages, out of
> vanity; everything else remained true. Now I will tell
> the whole story.

This version of the story is wildly different from the one told in *Graziella*: there is no tempest at sea, no lengthy stay with the simple fisherman's family, no reading of the novel *Paul et Virginie*. And yet Lamartine insists:

> The details that I am about to divulge are the only
> difference between the fiction of the novel and the

truth of the book. My youthful vanity could not allow
me to admit that my first love was for a cigarette
maker rather than a coral worker, which in fact she did
become later. Is there anything vanity will not color?

And now, having admitted it today, I can say that
the rest of the novel is completely correct. She was
just as young, as naive, as pure, as religious as I represented her in the novel. All the scenes are true. The
scenes and the actors are just as they were. The work
was less vulgar, and that is all.

The detail about his "youthful vanity" rings true; after he
had transfigured Graziella into Elvire in the early poems,
he asked Virieu to lie to Julie Charles about Elvire's social
status, as we saw earlier. But as for the rest of the tale of
Graziella, we are left to conclude that if much is contrived,
it is presumably done out of "vanity."

But there is one more important detail to bring into
the story, and that involves what appears to be plagiarism.
A novel titled *Charles Barimore* had been published anony-
mously in 1810, and though it had achieved no particular
acclaim, it was reprinted in 1843. Written by the Comte
de Forbin and republished by his son-in-law, the novel has
numerous scenes and details that are very close to those
in *Graziella*, including the tempest at sea, Procida and its
scenery, and the sentimental tone and atmosphere.[28] Two
newspapers accused Lamartine of plagiarism; he denied
it, claiming at one point that he had not read the book
and joking that if he had taken anything from the Comte
de Forbin, he would rather have had one of his paintings.
Forbin's son-in-law, the Comte de Marcellus, was a friend,
and there were evidently no hard feelings, so the entire
affair blew over. There is no conclusive proof of either
plagiarism or of Lamartine's innocence, but it is tempting

to speculate that he had in fact read the novel and unconsciously used it to frame his idealized narrative about the girl in the tobacco factory.

The Real Graziella

But the "whole story" that Lamartine presented in the *Mémoires* did not satisfy later readers and scholars, and the question of who Graziella really was, or whether she ever really existed, continued to fuel speculation and further research. (Might she have been, for example, a literary version of Valentine de Cessiat?) The definitive answer finally came with the work of Abel Verdier. Verdier established a set of facts that are yet farther from what is narrated in *Graziella* and farther from what is retold and supposedly corrected in the *Mémoires*. In the latter, Lamartine tells us there were two girls, Antoniella and Graziella, who both worked closely with his relative, Antoine Dareste de la Chavanne:

> There were two other people at the table: one was
> a female, around twenty or twenty-five years old,
> whom I learned later was called *Antoniella*. She was
> good-looking, but not remarkable; her familiarity with
> Monsieur de la Chavanne suggested a long employ-
> ment in the house; she was in charge of overseeing
> many of the girls who worked there making cigars;
> and the other was a ravishing young woman.

Verdier sifts the language used here with care, and putting it together with a phrase Lamartine used in a letter to Virieu, he concludes that Antoniella was in fact the mistress of Monsieur Antoine de la Chavanne (whose wife and family remained in France).[29] But the chain of clues leads Verdier to an even more startling revelation: there probably never was a second girl. There was only Antoniella.

And the love affair that ensued was with her, the twenty-something mistress of the factory director, not with an innocent teenage girl. Thus Antoniella was being unfaithful to Monsieur de la Chavanne, while Lamartine in turn was hardly acting the role of the well-behaved guest: the story is arguably a bit sordid, and far from the innocent pastoral that it became when Lamartine came to write about it.

Verdier was able to find out quite a lot about Antoniella. She was born on May 7, 1794, and thus was eighteen when she met Lamartine; the director, Antoine de la Chavanne, was fifty-one in 1811, so the ages of all the principals fit into the pattern of a conventional May–December fabliau. Antoniella was christened Maria Raffaela (her last name serving as a hint for the persona Lamartine would later assume for a different book, *Raphaël*), and her mother's name was Grazia. Children were often called by a diminutive version of their mother's name, and hence she might well have been nicknamed Graziella, though she usually went by the name Antoniella. Her death certificate lists her full name as Mariantonia Iacomino. She died, with the sacraments, on or about May 31, 1816, and was buried in Resina along the coast near Vesuvius in a cemetery that no longer exists. To know this is to know a great deal and to have a great many questions settled.

Further, we can also know roughly what she looked like, for Lamartine wrote in a letter to Virieu: "If I were to fall in love with someone, it would be the Duchesse de Broglie, whom I saw the other evening. Have you noticed how much she resembles Antoniella? I mean the way she carries herself, her eyes, and practically everything."[30] Albertine de Staël Holstein, Duchesse de Broglie (1797–1838), was the daughter of the great writer Madame de Staël; a number of portraits of her exist, including an especially fine, melancholic one by Ary Scheffer. The class difference between Mariantonia Iacomino and the Duchesse de Broglie was vast, of course, but the viewer can imagine something of what Lamartine's eighteen-year-old lover at the tobacco factory must have looked like. And the reality behind the idealized Graziella at last begins to take on a firmer outline.

Antoniella Iacomino did not die of a broken heart but of a chest ailment, probably tuberculosis (the same way Julie Charles died). And her death did not overwhelm the young Lamartine. We can infer the latter from a letter he wrote to Virieu in December 1816: at that point, Lamartine had not seen Antoniella for more than four years, but she survived in his poems under the name of Elvire. He tells Virieu, who is about to visit Julie Charles, to be discreet, and in doing so he casually drops the information that Antoniella had died:

> If she [Julie Charles] speaks to you about Antoniella, don't tell her who she was. Alas, I wrote to you some eight months ago about the death of Antoniella. She was dead of a chest ailment about fifteen months before that, and I knew nothing about it! And you didn't receive any word of it during that time. I'll tell you all about it.[31]

Virieu had been out of the country and not receiving his letters, so Lamartine here tries to catch him up quickly, but he garbles the dates, implying Antoniella had died at least a year earlier than she actually did. The emphasis inevitably marginalizes Antoniella and the news of her death, so that it is not the devastating news that it appears to be in *Graziella*. All this evidence suggests that the affair with Antoniella was simply another short-lived one and had not particularly mattered to the young man—at least, it was clearly not a deep, life-changing experience. But from such beginnings a legend begins to arise in the writing that began in 1844 during the return to Ischia.

Death and the Muse

Deborah Jenson speaks of Antoniella, with perhaps some sarcasm, as Lamartine's "ghostly plebian muse," noting that he disguises her class status in the poems (as he had Virieu do with Julie Charles) "for purposes of the narcissistic creation of the figure of the poet."[32] She goes on to quote from an early poem about the poet Parny, in which Lamartine exclaims, "Donnez-moi de sa voix l'accent mélodieux, / Mais surtout . . . une Eléonore!" (Give me the melodious accent of [Parny's] voice, / but above all . . . an Eleanor!) The implication is that such a muse is part of the poet's necessary equipment and that shortly after the affair with Antoniella he found he could use the memory of her as such a muse. That may be true for the Elvire poems, but by the time we get to 1844, another ghostly muse has been added to the original figure—Julie Charles, dead since 1817. And now in 1844, the presence of the young niece Valentine somehow calls up those ghosts, and the poet gives them all a new, idealized embodiment in the fisherman's granddaughter, Graziella.

The process is suggested, or rather replicated, by the coda sequence in *Graziella*, the sequence that includes the poem "Le Premier Regret." Lamartine describes the origin of the poem thus:

> One evening in the year 1830, having stopped inside
> a church in Paris, I saw people carrying the casket,
> draped with a white cloth, of a young girl. The casket
> made me think of Graziella. I hid myself behind a
> pillar, in the shadows. I recalled Procida, and I wept
> for a long while.
>
> My tears eventually stopped, but the clouds that
> overcast my thoughts during that sad burial service
> did not dissipate. I returned to my room in silence. I

went back over the memories that I have written in this long note, and then, in a single rush and weeping again the whole time, I wrote some verses titled "The First Regret." The poem is a feeble echo, at twenty years' distance, of a feeling that caused the springs of my heart to overflow for the first time. The emotion still lingers, like an inner nerve fiber that was injured long ago and has never really healed.

A constellation comes together here, with its key points being death, specifically the death of a young girl, and memory, a memory extended back over some eighteen years, all set within the interior of a church. The sequence of events ties the poem to the emotions unleashed by the moment in the church. Is it overstatement to say that the death of the young girl creates the poet?[33] If we go strictly by the sequence presented to us in *Graziella*, that was precisely the case. And if "Le Premier Regret" dates from 1830 (though we know Lamartine can be quite vague about dates), it will be another fourteen years until he fully tells the tale of the girl in the boat—the tale that he here calls "this long note."

A question worth asking, though, is what exactly does Lamartine's narrator "regret"? Is it Graziella's death, or the fact of death in general, represented by the nameless girl's coffin? Or is it rather something in himself, some lack? The latter is how Thomas G. Pavel reads the novel:

Lamartine refrains from analyzing the male character, who clearly suffers from what was known around 1830 as the *mal du siècle*, a condition that rendered upper-class young men indifferent to everything that might normally bring them happiness, especially love—although this condition strangely enhanced the sick man's ability to arouse love in the women around him.[34]

And indeed there is a strange lack of feeling in Lamartine's narrator, a lack he recognizes in himself. In real life, Lamartine did "regret" and miss Antoniella when he returned to France. In May 1812 he wrote to Virieu: "I have had no news from Naples. I miss that poor little Antoniella. I may never find another heart like hers. What the devil will become of her? My whole life I'm going to regret her, and there are tears in my eyes sometimes when I think of her."[35] But in the novel, he is far more concerned with class status, and about the possible mockery of his peers if they find out what sort of girl she is. The Lamartine of the novel, in other words, appears to be colder and shallower than the young Lamartine really was; it is as if the novelist writes that *mal du siècle*, or at least an emotional shallowness, into his younger self. The coda, then, with the poem brings the character to a certain emotional maturity and wholeness. When at the conclusion of the novel he asks our forgiveness, because "I have wept," it is as if this much-delayed feeling has an expiatory force.

Graziella and Intertextuality

And so, finally, we turn to the novelistic qualities of *Graziella*, recognizing at last that it is in fact a novel and not a memoir, at least not in any ordinary sense of that term. But the relationship between the book's fiction and its groundsprings in reality is complex and highly suggestive in terms of the creative process. It has a tangled relationship with biographical fact, and an equally complex relationship with other texts. First, there is *Charles Barimore*, as we have seen, which may in some unconscious way occupy some space in the substrata of *Graziella*'s conception and composition.

But equally important are the intertextualities that the novel evokes explicitly, especially the texts that Lamartine and his friend salvage and take with them to the fisherman's house: Ugo Foscolo's novel *The Last Letters of Jacopo Ortis*, Tacitus's history of Rome, and Bernardin de Saint-Pierre's *Paul et Virginie*. Of the three, Foscolo's is probably the least read today, but since the book was modeled directly on Goethe's *The Sorrows of Young Werther*, modern readers will be indirectly familiar with the tale of a passionate young man whose disappointments lead him to suicide. The difference is that Foscolo's novel is concerned with politics and specifically with the political situation in early nineteenth-century Italy, but both Goethe's Werther and Foscolo's Jacopo Ortis suffer from the Romantic malady of weltschmerz, of life in a world whose reality always falls short of the ideal.

In *Graziella*, Foscolo's book serves mainly to point out the curious lack of interest of their Italian listeners when Lamartine tries reading it to them:

> But we quickly saw that the scenes that had been so powerful for us [Lamartine and his friend Virieu] had no effect at all on these simple hearts. The passion for political liberty, which is always the aspiration of men of leisure, does not penetrate so deeply down into the people.
>
> These poor fishermen could not comprehend why Ortis was in such despair and why he killed himself, since he could have enjoyed all the real pleasures in life: to walk along with nothing pressing that he had to do, to see the sun, to love his mistress, and to pray to God along the river Brenta, with its grassy banks. "Why torment yourself," they asked, "over ideas that have no connection to your heart? Who cares whether it's the Austrians or the French who reign in Milan? Only a fool would get so upset over things like that." And they turned and stopped listening.

They get the same result when they read from Tacitus:

> As for Tacitus, they were even less interested. Empire or republic, the men killing each other, some to reign and others to avoid servitude, all the crimes committed for the throne, all those virtues practiced for the sake of glory, all those deaths for the sake of posterity—it all left them cold. The grand storms of history played themselves out too far above their heads for them to be affected by them. For them, such things were like the thunder one hears up on the mountain, which can be ignored because it will only affect the heights and would not so much as fill the sail of the fisherman or ever touch the house of the farmer.

To what extent this is condescension, the reader must judge. But in considering these passages we ought to recall that Lamartine remained acutely interested in the reading habits of the lower classes, and he thought France was on the verge of a kind of revolution in literature; he supported a number of worker poets, including women, and wrote or planned works designed to appeal to the working class. In the preface to his novel *Geneviève* (1850), set up as a dialogue between himself and the working-class woman poet Reine Lagarde, he forecasts that within a decade there will be people's journalism, philosophy, literature; in the past, he declares, it was an honor for a writer to address the monarch or a noble, but in the future the honor will be in writing for the people.[36]

Foscolo and Tacitus fail to interest the simple fisherman's family. But the book that does resonate with them is the novel *Paul et Virginie*: "We had discovered the chord that pulses in unison with the heart in all people, in all ages, and in all social conditions, the sympathetic chord, the universal one, the one that contains within its single sound the eternal truth of art: nature, love, and God." The family, and especially Graziella herself, become positively rapt by Lamartine's improvised translation of the book:

> Her wide-open eyes stared now at the book, now at
> my lips, from which the story was flowing, and some-
> times at the gap between my lips and the book, as if
> she were seeking the invisible spirit that was commu-
> nicating to me. I heard her uneven breath stopping
> and starting, following the rhythm of the drama; she
> sounded at times like someone climbing a mountain
> and pausing from time to time to catch her breath.
> By the time I reached the middle of the tale, the poor
> child had lost all her half-wild reserve with me. I could
> feel the warmth of her breathing on my hands. Her
> hair brushed my face. Two or three teardrops ran
> down her cheeks and fell, making tiny stains on the
> pages, right beside my fingers.

The illiterate Graziella reacts to the reading as if it were some kind of magic. When Lamartine (somewhat cruelly) tells the group he will stop reading for the night, she reacts as if the book were alive and she could somehow command it: "She tore the book out of my hands. She opened it, as if by sheer force of will she would be able to decipher the characters. She spoke to it, she kissed it. She then placed it respectfully back onto my knees, raising her joined hands to me like a supplicant."

The moment is curiously similar to a moment that occurs in a number of slave narratives, what Henry Louis Gates Jr. calls the trope of the talking book. The slave recognizes a power in the printed word, but being illiterate he or she cannot yet understand how to harness that power. For Gates, the trope, in leading to an eventual mastery of the book, is also suggestive of the slave narrator's transformation from one kind of subjectivity to another, of becoming a new kind of person, and Graziella too is transformed by her encounter with the book.[37] But in her case, the transformation is immediate and is literalized, physicalized:

> Her face, normally so serene and smiling, though in an austere way, had now, from the story's passion and tenderness, taken on suddenly some of its wildness and pathos. It was as if some subtle alteration had turned a beautiful marble statue into flesh and tears. The girl felt her soul, which had lain asleep within her until now, begin to awaken, through the soul of Virginie. She seemed to have aged by six years or so in the course of the past half an hour. Her forehead now was tinted with the stormy hues of passion, as were the white purities of her eyes and cheeks. It was like a calm and sheltered pond when the sun, wind, and shadows come to battle with it for the first time.

The statue reference here repeats the earlier note that Graziella was listening to the reading in the posture of the much-admired statue known as *The Dying Gaul.* In the course of the reading, she first becomes statue-like and then is liberated from marble into "flesh and tears." The metamorphosis is also from childhood to adulthood, from innocence to a passionate yet chaste eroticism.

The story of Bernardin de Saint-Pierre's 1787 novel *Paul et Virginie* concerns two children from different social castes raised together in the pastoral innocence of an island, far from the corruption and social divisions that civilization imposes. Bernardin de Saint-Pierre was a friend and disciple of Rousseau, and the perfection of human life in a "natural" setting is pure Rousseauism. The two children grow up and into a natural and profound love for each other. But at last Virginie's aunt recalls her to France; her absence drives Paul to near despair. Finally after two years away she returns to the island, but her ship is wrecked within sight of the land; Paul witnesses her drowning.

The function of *Paul et Virginie* within Lamartine's novel is complex, but even this brief plot summary indicates many points of contact—the idyllic natural setting, the caste distinction, the threat or menace that "civilization" or the return to France denotes. Beyond those connections, though, we see that the earlier novel actually furthers the plot in *Graziella*, turning the character Graziella from a childlike friend or sister into a young adult potential lover. As Marius-François Guyard puts it, the earlier novel is much more than a source; it actually becomes a character in the later one.[38] And Jillian Heydt-Stevenson's study of the interplay between the two novels argues that Lamartine is developing a theme concerning art's universality: "Lamartine is trying to dramatize through the thingness of the book Graziella's attraction to the power of art, and especially the power that suffering, mediated through art, has on humans. . . . [This idea] arises from Lamartine's political commitment to democratic liberalism, a commitment to educating the poor."[39] Lamartine or, rather, Lamartine's narrator likewise has apparently had an important relationship with the earlier novel: "I had read the book so often that I had it more or less by heart. Our long stay in Italy had familiarized me with the language, so finding the right expressions came easily to me, and words rolled off my tongue as if I were speaking in my maternal language." The latter point strains credibility, but we are asked to believe that the book and the reader had so melded together that translation—into a language he had barely had time to learn—was easy and natural. The earlier book again takes on an almost magical life here, as magical for Lamartine as it had been for Graziella, though in different ways, and it suggests a great deal about Lamartine's Romantic ideas concerning reading and the power of literature.[40]

Translation in the sense that Lamartine uses it here (in the narrator's effortless improvisational translation of *Paul et Virginie*) is connected to a pattern of ideas that he develops in his poetry and other writings.[41] The poet is a translator by virtue of the fact that poetry contacts a higher, mysterious realm of truth beyond the powers of ordinary people and beyond the powers of ordinary language to express. In *Raphaël*, as we saw, the letters between Raphaël and his lover were examples, in that they needed to force a way through ordinary language to reach the higher truth of the love they wanted to express: "In these letters, there was neither beginning nor end, nor middle, nor grammar, nor anything like what one would ordinarily call style."[42] Poetry works in a similar way, Lamartine suggests, through symbols and violations of the norms of ordinary discourse, becoming a translation of the higher, more mysterious reality. As Roger Pearson puts it: "Poetry is also the double-saying of a repetition: of repetition in the form of translation, and of repetition in the form of an endless resaying. Poetry is translation in that the human being speaks intelligibly in the language of the here and now about an unintelligible and inexpressible realm beyond the reach of mere mimesis."[43] Lamartine's narrator of *Graziella* should be seen in this light, with his rapid accession of perfect Neapolitan dialect and his easy natural translation of Bernardin de Saint-Pierre's French, together with his long acquaintance with this almost holy book, all suggesting an image of the poet/artist in a state of inspiration. In *Graziella* the reading aloud of *Paul et*

Virginie is a dramatized instance of this kind of resaying, this translation.

As Graziella's posture echoed the statue of *The Dying Gaul*, so Lamartine's reading echoes the ancient work of the inspired oral poet.[44] Echoes of ancient myth abound in the novel, with constant reminders that the islanders, particularly the fisherman's family, trace their roots back to Greece. The local peasants wear Greek-influenced clothing as a visual reminder of that ancestry. The tempest at sea, the magical isle, the appearance of the virginal enchantress, Graziella's flight from home during the stormy night, and the divine intervention of the Madonna—all these, and so much more, are the material of epic and of romance. "Every family is a history, and even a poem, for the one who knows how to read it," says Lamartine of the fisherman's family, and *Graziella* may be seen as a lesson in reading. I refer not only to the specific scene of reading *Paul et Virginie*, important as that is, but also to the whole of the novel. We have seen that this story, so anxious to pass itself off as memoir, is entirely constructed, entirely a work of imagination. Imagination working on memory, imagination learning how to read the truth of memory: this is the importance of the phenomenon of *Graziella*, both the book and its long, twisting process of gestation. That process begins fitfully, with the early Elvire poems, the poet trying to construct a muse. Then it is lived out, in the love affair with the married, dying Julie Charles, resulting in more poetry (some of it, like "Le Lac," reaching the level of masterpiece). And then, at the age of fifty-four, a political career on the rise and age beginning to take its toll on the man, Lamartine takes his return trip to Ischia in the company of Valentine, and now the memories and the muses and all his poetic impulses combine to fashion a personal myth, an origin story. "Every scene in it is true,"

Lamartine insists: evidently, this is the truth of myth, the truth of translated reality.

As we have seen, all this was in the cauldron during Lamartine's year of rejuvenation, 1844, but he put literature aside—or, rather, these particular literary projects—in order to return to politics, only returning to the tale of Graziella in early 1849, when, as he must have known, his political career was essentially over. So it was in those early months of 1849 that *Confidences* saw print, as did *Raphaël*. But what has lasted out of all the writing that followed was the short interpolated tale from the middle of the volume of *Confidences*, the "episode" titled *Graziella*. Verdier notes that between Lamartine's death and 1895, 106,000 copies of *Graziella* were sold in France—a phenomenal number for the nineteenth century.[45] And there were further translations—into English, German, Italian, Spanish, Turkish, and of course Italian (more than twenty-four different Italian translations, in fact). The story has been adapted into opera three times and into film three times, in 1917, 1926 (featuring the poet Antonin Artaud as Cecco), and 1954. For all the fabrication that went into what initially passed for a memoir, there remains a strange purity hovering around *Graziella* like an aureole. To use Émile Henriot's phrase, it has become something of a breviary of the heart—one of those books, like Eugène Fromentin's *Dominique* or Sainte-Beuve's *Volupté* or, indeed, Bernardin de Saint-Pierre's *Paul et Virginie*, that tells a simple and sentimental tale so perfectly that the book transcends its own limitations and weaknesses and becomes a myth of perfect, innocent love.[46] But never such innocence again: the closest thing to such a novel that the twentieth century could provide, a tale of young love and the coming of age of the male narrator, is one that announces its difference in its very title: Raymond Radiguet's *The Devil in the Flesh* (*Le Diable au corps*).

Graziella

I

When I was eighteen, my family entrusted me to the care of a relative whose business affairs called her to Tuscany, where she went accompanied by her husband.[1] It was an opportunity for me to travel and to get away from that dangerous kind of boredom that sets in at home and in provincial towns, where the soul's early passions become corrupted for lack of an object. I set off with all the enthusiasm of a child about to see the curtain raised on the most splendid scenes of nature and life.

The Alps, which ever since my childhood I had been able to see far off, when I stood on the hillside of Milly,[2] their eternal snows glistening on the distant horizon; the sea, which had been imprinted on my soul in striking imagery from travelers and poets; the Italian sky whose heat and serenity I had already, so to speak, breathed in from the pages of *Corinne*[3] and from the poetry of Goethe: "Do you know the place, that land where the myrtle blossoms?"[4] And the still-standing monuments from Roman antiquity, images of which filled my thoughts from my recent studies; liberty itself; that distance that casts a kind of aura over faraway things; adventures and the accidental events that are sure to occur on a long journey, already visualized in the youthful imagination, already sources of pleasure and of savor; a new language, new faces, new customs, all hinting at an entirely new world—all of this was fascination to my spirit. I was in a prolonged state of euphoria during the endless days awaiting our departure. That exhilaration, reinvigorated every day by the magnificent scenes of nature in Savoy, in Switzerland, on the banks of Lake Geneva, on the Simplon glacier, by Lake Como, by Milan, and by Florence never really left me until my return.

The business that my traveling companions had in Livorno became prolonged indefinitely, and there was talk of sending me back to France without having seen Rome or Naples. This was equivalent to murdering my dream before it had a chance to be born. I rebelled inwardly at the idea. I wrote to my father for his permission to continue traveling on my own in Italy and without waiting for his reply, which I could hardly expect to be favorable, I resolved to avoid disobedience by engineering a fait accompli. "If he forbids it," I said to myself, "his letter will have arrived too late. I will be reprimanded, but I will also be forgiven; I will go back home, but I will have been somewhere!" I examined my very limited finances, but I counted on a relative of my mother's who lived in Naples and who would surely not begrudge me the bit of money I would need for my return. One clear evening I slipped out of Livorno, on board the coach to Rome.

I spent the winter there alone, in a little room on a side street that emptied onto the Piazza di Spagna, in the home of a Roman painter and his family, who took me in as a boarder. My appearance, my youth, my enthusiasm, and my isolation in an unknown country had combined to interest one of my traveling companions on the road between Florence and Rome. We soon bonded together in friendship. He was a handsome young man about my age. He appeared to be the son or nephew of the famous singer David, who was then the foremost tenor in the concert halls of Italy. David also traveled with us. He was a man of advanced age, and he was on his way to sing for the last time at the Saint-Charles in Naples.[5]

David acted like a father to me, and his young companion showed me endless consideration and little favors, to which I responded with the warmth and naïveté of youth. We had scarcely arrived in Rome before he and I had already become inseparable. In those days, the coach took no fewer than three days to get from Florence to Rome. In the inns, my new friend acted as my translator; at table, he served me first; in the coach, he saw to it that I had the most comfortable spot, and if I fell asleep, I could be sure that I would awaken with my head on his shoulder as a pillow.

When I got down from the coach for the long up-hill walks in Tuscany or in the Sabine Hills, he came with me, telling me about the countryside, naming the villages, pointing out the monuments. He would pick beautiful flowers, and he bought fine figs and grapes along our route; he would fill my hands and my cap with the fruits. David seemed to observe with pleasure the affection his companion felt for the young stranger. They would sometimes exchange a smile as they looked at me, a smile of intelligence, delicacy, and good nature.

When we arrived at Rome at nightfall, I naturally stayed in the same inn that they did. I was led to my room; later I awoke to the sound of my young friend knocking at my door and inviting me to breakfast. I hurried to dress and rushed downstairs to the room where the travelers were reunited. I went to find my young companion and shake his hand, but I looked in vain at the faces of the group gathered there, and as I did so, they all broke out in laughter. Instead of the son or nephew of David, I saw next to David the charming figure of a young Roman girl elegantly dressed, her black hair held back by a headband in front and pinned up by two golden pins in the back, in the way that the peasant girls of Tivoli still wear their hair. It was my friend who, having arrived at Rome, had reverted to her proper clothing and sex.

I should have suspected something from the gentleness of her glances and the grace of her smile. But I had had no suspicions whatsoever. "A change of clothes is not a change of heart," the lovely Roman said to me, blushing. "Only, you must not sleep on my shoulder anymore, and instead of my giving you flowers, you should give them to me. This adventure should teach you not to trust in the appearances of friendship that people may show you in the future; the reality may be something very different."

The young woman was a singer, a protégé and favorite of David. The aging singer brought her everywhere with him, dressing her in men's clothing to avoid gossip along the road. He was more like a father to her than a protector and was not at all jealous of the sweet and innocent little familiarities that he had allowed to grow up between us.

II

David and his student spent several weeks in Rome. The day after our arrival, she again dressed as a man and took me to see St. Peter's first, then the Coliseum, and then Frascati, Tivoli, Albano; I was thus spared the wearisome repetitions of the hired guides who dissect the corpse of Rome for tourists and who, chanting in monotone their litany of names and dates, drown out one's own impressions, weigh down our thoughts, and detour us from the beautiful feelings that such sights can arouse. Camilla was no savant, but having been born in Rome she knew by instinct the finest sights and prospects, the ones that had been most striking to her since her childhood.

She escorted me almost by intuition to the best places

at the best times of day in order to contemplate the ruins of the ancient city: in the morning, beneath the pines of the great domes of Monte Pincio; in the evening, beneath the colonnades of St. Peter's; in the moonlight, within the mute circle of the Coliseum; on beautiful autumn days, in Albano, or Frascati, or the temple of the Sibyl, amid the rustle and spray of the Tivoli waterfall. She was cheerful and playful, like a statue of eternal Youth standing amid the ruins of time and death. She danced on the Tomb of Caecilia Metella, and while I sat daydreaming on a rock, she made her voice echo under the sinister vaults of Diocletian's Palace.

In the evening we would come back to town, our cart filled with flowers and bits of debris from statues, to rejoin David, whose affairs kept him in Rome and who took us at day's end to his box in the theater. The girl singer, a few years older than I, never showed any feelings for me beyond those of a somewhat tender friendship. I was too timid to show her any of my own; and in fact, I did not have any strong feelings, despite her beauty and my own youth. Her men's clothing, her masculine ease, the male tone of her contralto voice, and the freedom of her manners all made such an impression on me that I never saw in her anything other than a handsome young man, a comrade, and a friend.

III

When Camilla had gone, I stayed on in Rome entirely alone, with no letters of introduction and without any acquaintances apart from the sights, the monuments, and the ruins to which she had introduced me. The old painter with whom I lodged only came out of his atelier on Sundays to go to Mass with his wife and daughter, a girl of sixteen who worked just as hard as he did.[6] Their house was like a monastery in which the labor of the artist was only interrupted by frugal repasts and prayer.

In the evening, when the last rays of the sun were fading through the high windows of the poor painter's room, and when the bells of the neighboring monasteries were tolling the Ave Maria, that harmonious farewell bid to the day throughout Italy, the family's only relaxation was to say the rosary together, intoning their prayers in a half-chant until their voices, drooping into sleepiness, began to sink and subside into a vague, monotone murmur, in the same way that a tossing wave comes to rest on a beach, when the wind and the night both fall.

I loved this pious, quiet evening scene, the working day reaching its conclusion in that hymn of the three souls rising up into the sky, putting the day to rest. It brought back memories of my family's house, where our mother, too, would bring us all together in the evening to pray, sometimes in her room and sometimes in the walkways of the little garden at Milly, in the last moments of sunset. And finding here again the same customs, the same behaviors, the same religion, I felt almost as if by being in the home of this foreign family I were back in my own family home. I have never seen a more reverent, more solitary, more hardworking, and more sanctified life than the one I saw in the Roman painter's house.

The painter had a brother.[7] This brother did not live with him; he taught Italian to foreigners of means who came to spend their winters in Rome. He was more than a language teacher, however; he was a Roman man of letters of the first rank. Still young, strikingly handsome, with old-fashioned manners, he had been a leading figure in the attempts at revolution that Roman republicans had made as they tried to restore liberty to their land. He was a people's tribune, a Cola di Rienzo of his era.[8] During that brief resurrection of ancient Rome, sustained by the French and suppressed by General Mack and the Neapolitans, he had played a major role, speaking to the people at the Capitol, displaying the flag of independence, and occupying one of the chief posts of the republic.[9] Pursued, persecuted, and imprisoned when the reaction came, he was saved only upon the arrival of the French, who saved the republicans but confiscated the republic.

This Roman adored the France of the Revolution, and the France of the *philosophes*; he detested the Emperor and the Empire. For him, and for all liberal Italians, Bonaparte was like the Caesar of liberty. Still young myself, I shared those sentiments. The similarity of our views soon became clear to us. Seeing the enthusiasm, both juvenile and classic, with which I responded to the accents of liberty when we read together the incendiary works of the poet Monti, or the republican scenes of Alfieri, he saw that he could be open with me, and I became less his pupil and more his friend.[10]

IV

The proof that liberty is the divine ideal of humankind is that it shapes the first dreams of youth; the passion for liberty only fades in our soul when the heart withers and the mind decays or grows dispirited. There is no soul of twenty that is not republican. There is no withered heart that is not servile.

How many times did my teacher and I sit together on the hill by the Palazzo Pamphili, from whence one can see Rome, its domes and ruins, its Tiber creeping filthy, silent, and ashamed beneath the arches of the Ponte Rotto, and from whence one can hear the plaintive murmurings of the city's fountains, and the almost silent footsteps of its people, mutely walking down its deserted streets! How many times did we weep the bitter tears that tyranny always arouses everywhere in this world, this world that sees philosophy and liberty barely being born in France or Italy before they are crushed, betrayed, and suppressed everywhere! What curses did we mutter against that tyrant over the human spirit, that crowned soldier who had been born out of revolution, only to use his strength to destroy that very revolution that had sought to liberate the people from ancient prejudices and ancient servitude! This period marked the beginning of the emancipation of my spirit, and of that intellectual hatred for that hero of the century, a hatred both deeply felt and carefully thought out, and which later reflection and years have only justified, despite the flatterers of his memory.

V

It was under the sway of such impressions that I studied Rome, its history and monuments. I would go out alone in the morning, before the bustle of the city could distract me from my contemplations. Under my arm I carried the historians, the poets, the describers of Rome. I would go off to sit or to wander through the deserted ruins of the Forum, the Coliseum, the Roman countryside. By turns I gazed, I read, I thought. I made a serious study of Rome, but a study based on action. This was my first course in history. Antiquity, instead of being a bore, became for me a feeling. I followed only my own interests, having no other objective or plan. I went where chance, or my feet, took me. I progressed from ancient Rome to modern Rome, from the Pantheon to the palace of Leo X, from the house of Horace on the Tiber to the house of Raphael. Poets, painters, historians, great men—all of them passed confusedly before my eyes; I only paused when something on that particular day took my attention.

Around eleven o'clock, I would go back to my little room in the painter's house for my meal. I would continue reading as I ate a bit of bread and cheese at my worktable. For a drink I would have a glass of milk, and then I would work, take notes, write until dinnertime. The wife and daughter of my host prepared dinner for us themselves. After eating, I would go out to wander again until night came. Some hours of conversation with the painter's family and prolonged reading well into the night—these brought my peaceful days to their close. I felt no need for any further society. In fact I delighted in my isolation. Rome and my soul were enough for me. In this way I passed the whole long winter, from October until the next April, without a single day of restlessness or boredom. It was the memory of those days that led me, some ten years later, to write certain poems on the Tiber.

VI

Now when I think back over all my impressions of Rome, I find two that almost erase all the others, or at least dominate them: the Coliseum, that great work of the people of Rome, and St. Peter's, the masterpiece of Catholicism. The Coliseum is the gigantic trace of a superhuman people who erected, for their own pride and for their own ferocious pleasures, monuments capable of containing an entire nation—monuments rivaling, in their scope and in their duration, the very works of nature. The Tiber will have dried up to nothing more than mud, and the Coliseum will continue to dominate over it.

St. Peter's is the work of an idea, or a religion, of the entirety of humanity from a certain epoch. This is no edifice destined to house an ignoble people. This is a temple destined to house all philosophy, all prayers, all the grandeur, and all the thought of humankind. Its walls seem to rise up and grow larger, no longer on a human scale but on the scale of God. Only Michelangelo truly understood Catholicism, and he gave to St. Peter's its most sublime and its most complete expression. St. Peter's is truly an apotheosis in stone, the monumental transfiguration of the religion of Christ.

The architects of the gothic cathedrals were sublime barbarians. Only Michelangelo was a true philosopher in his conception of the cathedral. St. Peter's is the philosophy of Christianity, from which the divine architect has chased away the shadows, and into whose interior space he has brought beauty, symmetry, and inexhaustible waves of light. The incomparable beauty of St. Peter's in Rome lies in its being a temple designed to clothe the idea of God in all its splendor.

Christianity could perish and St. Peter's would remain the universal, eternal, rational temple of whatever religion succeeded the cult of Christ—provided that the new religion was worthy of humanity and of God! It is the most abstract temple that human genius, inspired by an idea of the divine, has ever constructed here below. When you enter, it is not clear whether you are entering an ancient or a modern temple; no detail offends the eye, and no symbol distracts the mind; people of all religions enter there with the same respect. We sense that this is a temple that could only be inhabited by the idea of God, and that no other idea could possibly fill it.

Change the priest, remove the altar, take down the paintings, remove the statues: nothing has changed; it remains the house of God! Or, to put it another way, St. Peter's is the great symbol of that eternal Christianity that, carrying within its morality and its holiness the seeds of all successive religious development, of all religious thought in all centuries and among all peoples, opens itself up to reason to the degree that God grants it light, and that communicates with God in the light, that enlarges and extends itself to fit the proportions of the ceaselessly expanding human spirit, receiving all the peoples of the earth in the unity of adoration, making of all the various divine forms one single God, of all times one single religion, and of all peoples one single humanity.

Michelangelo is the Moses of monumental Catholicism, as it will one day be understood. He has crafted an imperishable arch leading into future eras, the Pantheon of divinized Reason.

VII

Having finally sated myself with Rome, I wanted to go on and see Naples. What attracted me above all were the tomb of Virgil and the birthplace of Tasso. Countries and men have always blended together for me. Naples is Virgil and Tasso. To me it seemed as if they lived there only yesterday and that the ashes of their hearths were still warm. I could already see in my mind's eye Pausilippo and Sorrento, Vesuvius and the sea, through the atmosphere created by the beautiful, tender geniuses of those men.

I left for Naples toward the end of March.[11] I traveled by post chaise with a French businessman who was looking for a companion to share the costs of the trip. Not too far from Velletri, we encountered the Rome-to-Naples mail coach overturned by the roadside and riddled with bullets. The postman, a postilion, and two horses had all been killed. The dead men had just been carried off to a nearby farmstead. Ripped-open envelopes and scraps of letters still fluttered around us in the wind. The brigands had fled by the Abruzzo road. French cavalry and infantry, encamped at Terracina, were pursuing them among the rocks. We could hear gunshots, and up on the

mountainside we could see little white puffs from the ri-
fles. All the way along the road we encountered postings
of French and Neapolitan troops. And so it was that we
made our entry into the kingdom of Naples.

This brigandage had a political aspect. Joachim Murat
reigned at the time. The Calabrians were actively resisting;
King Ferdinand, who had retreated to Sicily, subsidized
the guerrilla chieftains in the mountains.[12] The famous
Fra Diavolo fought at the head of one of these groups.[13]
Their exploits were assassinations. We only found order
and security when we finally got inside Naples itself.

I arrived on the first of April. A few days after that, I
was joined by a young man of about my age, my closest
friend from school, as much brother as friend. His name
was Aymon de Virieu. His life and mine were so closely entwined, from his childhood until his death, that we
were, so to speak, parts of each other, and I speak of him
as often as I speak of myself.[14]

Episode

I

At Naples, I led a contemplative life much like the one I
led in Rome, at the old painter's home on the Piazza di
Spagna; the only difference was that instead of spending
my days wandering among the debris of antiquity, I now
spent them wandering along the shores or over the waves
of the gulf of Naples. In the evenings I would return to
the old monastery where, thanks to the hospitality of my
mother's relative, I inhabited a little cell just under the
roof, with a balcony festooned with pots of flowers and
creeping plants, and a view of the sea, Vesuvius, Castellammare, and Sorrento.[15]

When the morning horizon was clear, I could see the

glistening white of Tasso's house, suspended like a swan's nest atop a cliff side of yellow rock, splashed by the waves. The sight was ravishing to me. The light of that house shone down into the depths of my soul. It was like the lightning stroke of glory bursting from afar over my youth and my obscurity. I recalled the Homeric scene that was that great man's life when, released from prison but still pursued by small minds and the calumnies of the great, his very genius—his only wealth—ridiculed and besmirched, he returned to Sorrento to seek a little rest, a little tenderness, or a little pity and, disguised as a beggar he came to his sister in order to tempt her and to see if she—if she alone—would recognize the one she had once so loved.

"She recognizes him at once," says the simple biographer, "despite his sickly pallor, his beard grown white, and his ragged cloak. She throws herself into his arms with more tenderness and mercy than she would have had she encountered her brother dressed in the golden robes of Ferrara's courtiers. Her voice is stifled by sobs for a long while; she presses her brother closely to her heart. She washes his feet and brings his father's cloak to him, and then prepares him a festive meal. But neither he nor she could so much as touch the dishes they were served, their hearts were so full of tears; and they spent the day weeping together, saying nothing, looking out at the sea, and recalling their childhood."

II

One day, toward the beginning of summer, at that period when the gulf of Naples, surrounded by hills with their white houses, and surrounded by rocks carpeted with creeping vines, and vaulted above by a sky only less clear than its own waters, looks like an ancient green goblet brimming with foam; the young vine shoots spread out and decorate the coves and the shorelines; this is the season when the fishermen of Pausilippo, their huts perched upon the rocks and their nets spread out on the beaches of fine sand, push off from the shore with confidence, heading out to fish all night two or three leagues off into the sea, almost as far as the beaches of Capri, of Procida, of Ischia, and the gulf of Gaeta.

Some of them take resin torches with them, which they then light to trick the fish. The fish come up to the light, believing it is the light of dawn. A child bends silently out over the boat's prow, his torch hanging down over the waves, while the fisherman, gazing down into the depths of the water, tries to make out his prey and cast his net over it. The flame of these torches, red as a cinder in a furnace, is reflected in long furrows over the nap of the sea, like the long rays of light cast by streetlamps. The undulation of the waves makes the light move and shift, prolonging the glare and reflecting it from wave to wave, as bright on the most distant wave as it is on the nearest.

III

My friend and I often spent whole hours sitting on a reef or on the wet ruins of the palace of Queen Joanna, watching those fantastic lights and envying the fishermen their carefree, nomadic lives.[16]

After several months' residence in Naples, and because of our frequent encounters with men of the people in the course of our days spent both in the countryside and by the sea, we had familiarized ourselves with their language, sonorous and accented, in which gestures and the facial expression say more than the actual words. Philosophers by intuition, and wearied of all of life's vain struggles—though before we had actually experienced them—we often felt envious of those cheerful *lazzaroni* who seem to cover the beaches and the docks of Naples, who spend

their days sleeping in the shade of their little boats, listening to improvised verses from their strolling poets,
and in the evenings dancing the tarantella with the young
girls of their class beneath some arbor by the shore of the
sea.[17] We knew their characters, their habits, and their
ways much better than those of elegant society, where we
chose never to go. We liked this life, and as to those fever-
ish movements of the soul that burn up the imaginations
of young men until the destined hour that will call upon
them, we let them remain sleeping within us.

My friend was twenty; I was eighteen: we were both
therefore at the age when one is permitted to confuse
dreams with realities. We decided that we would become
better acquainted with those fishermen, and that we would
embark with them in order to lead the kind of life they did
for a few days. Those humid, luminous nights spent beneath the sail, rocked gently by the waves under that deep,
starry sky—this seemed to us one of the most mysterious
pleasures nature had to offer, one that we had to seize and
experience, even if it were only for the pleasure of being
able to tell about it later.

Utterly free, without needing to account for our com-
ings and goings to anyone, we put our plan into practice
the next day. Walking along the beach of Margellina,
which extends from Virgil's tomb to the foot of Monte
Pausilippo, and where the Neapolitan fishermen haul up
their boats and mend their nets, we came upon a robust
old man. He was loading his equipment into his fishing
boat, which was painted in bright colors and sported a
little carved image of St. Francis atop its stern. A twelve-
year-old child, his only rower, was just then loading two
loaves and a cheese with a thick rind, golden and glittering
like the pebbles on the beach, along with some figs and an
earthenware water jug.

The look of the old man and the boy appealed to us.

We struck up a conversation with them. The fisherman broke into a smile when we proposed coming along to sea with him as oarsmen.

"You don't have the kind of callused hands you'd need to manage the oars," he said to us. "Those white hands of yours are made for holding quill pens, not wood: it would be a shame to roughen them up at sea."

My friend replied, "We are young, and we want the chance to try out all the different ways of life before choosing one. Yours appeals to us, because you lead it on the sea and under the open sky."

"You're right," said the old boatman. "It's a life that makes the heart content and makes the spirit trust in the saints' protection. The fisherman is directly under the protection of heaven. The man never knows where the wave or the wind will come from. The laborer has his plane and his file right in his own hand, and the rich man's fate lies in the favor of the king, but the boat is in the hand of God."

This pious philosophy of the fisherman only attracted us all the more to the idea of embarking with him. After a long resistance, he finally consented. We settled on giving him two *carline* a day as payment for our apprenticeships and our food.

These arrangements all agreed to, he sent the boy off to Margellina to pick up additional provisions of bread, hard cheese, and fruit. At nightfall, we assisted in getting the boat onto the waves, and we pushed off.

IV

The first night was delicious. The sea was as calm as a lake in Switzerland surrounded by mountains. As we proceeded farther out to sea, we watched the little tongues of fire in the windows of the palace and the docks of Naples slowly sink and become buried beneath the dark line of the horizon. Only the lighthouses indicated where the coastline was. Their light paled next to the bright column of fire shooting upward from the crater of Vesuvius. As the fisherman cast his net and pulled it back in, and as the half-sleeping boy let his torch waver over the water, we rowed a little now and then to give the boat a bit of movement, and we listened in delight to the sonorous dripping of the water as it rustled off our oars and fell harmoniously into the sea, like pearls into a silver basin.

We had long passed the Pausilippo point, crossed the gulf of Pozzuoli and that of Baiae, and we had passed through the canal of the gulf of Gaeta, between the cape of Miseno and the island of Procida. We were now fully out to sea; sleep began to overcome us. We lay down on our benches, next to the boy.

The fisherman stretched out the heavy canvas sailcloth over us, and we fell asleep thus on the waves, rocked gently by a sea that scarcely tilted the mast. When we awoke, it was broad daylight.

A bright sun cast vivid, ruby-like reflections on the waves, shining down too on the white houses of an unknown shoreline. A light breeze came from that shore, fluttering the sail over our heads and propelling us past cove after cove, rock after rock. This was the serrated, ragged coastline of the charming island of Ischia, which I was soon to inhabit and come to love. Now it appeared to me for the first time, floating in the sunlight, rising up out of the sea, losing itself in the blue of the sky, blossoming there like the dream of a poet in a light sleep on a midsummer's night . . .

V

The island of Ischia, seated between the gulf of Gaeta and the gulf of Naples, and separated from the island of

Procida by only a narrow canal, consists entirely of a single steep mountain whose white, blasted peak seems to plunge jagged teeth into the sky. Its abrupt flanks, crisscrossed by valleys, ravines, and the beds of powerful rivers, are covered from top to bottom with the dark green of chestnut trees. The plateaus closest to the sea, running down to the waves below, support huts, rustic villas, and little villages half-covered by climbing vines. Each of these villages has its own *marine*—which is what they call the tiny port where the island's fishing boats are moored, and where a few masts bearing Latin-style sails sway.[18] The yardarms touch and mingle with the tree branches and the vines.

Not a one of those little houses suspended on the slopes of the mountain—hidden within a ravine, perched pyramid-like atop a plateau, projecting out from one of the capes, tilted up against a great chestnut tree, shadowed by a group of pines, surrounded by white pathways, and festooned with trailing vines—there is not one of these that would disappoint a poet's dream, or a lover's, of the ideal dwelling.

Our eyes never tired of the sight. The coastline abounded in fish. The fisherman had had a good night. We came up to one of the island's small coves to fill up our water from a nearby spring and to rest among the rocks. When sunset came, we returned to Naples, reclining on our rowing benches. A square sail, placed across the prow on a small mast and tended by the boy, was all it took for us to ride along the beaches of Procida and the cape of Miseno, and to churn up foam from the surface of the water beneath our skiff.

The old fisherman and the boy, aided by us, pulled the boat up onto the sand and carried the baskets of fish into the cellar of the little house they inhabited beneath the rocks of Margellina.

VI

The following days saw us happily pursuing our new profession. We skimmed all over the sea around Naples. We followed the wind wherever it took us. Thus, we visited the isle of Capri, our imaginations still haunted by the sinister memory of Tiberius; Cumae and its temples, half-hidden beneath the foliage of dense bay trees and wild fig trees; Baiae and its bleak beaches, which seemed to have aged and whitened like the bones of those Romans to whose youth and pleasures they had borne witness; Portici and Pompeii, smiling beneath the lava and the cinders of Vesuvius; Castellammare, with its high, black forests of bay and wild chestnut trees, tinting with a dark green the ever-murmuring waters of its harbor. The old boatman knew the families of fishermen like him everywhere, and we always enjoyed hospitality whenever the sea was rough and we were prevented from returning to Naples.

For two months we lived without ever setting foot in an inn. We lived outdoors, with the people, and living the frugal life of the people. We became of the people ourselves, in order to be closer to nature. We dressed almost the same as they did. We spoke their language, and the simplicity of their ways seemed somehow to communicate the innocence of their feelings.

And this transformation came at very little cost to my friend and me. Raised, both of us, in the countryside during the storms of the Revolution, which had battered and dispersed our families, we had already lived in our childhood years very much the peasant life. For him, it was in the mountains of Grésivaudan, with a nurse who took him in while his mother had been imprisoned; for me, it was among the hills of Mâconnais, in a small rustic house where my father and mother had gathered us together, and that formed our little nest hidden away from danger. Between the shepherd or laborer of our mountains and the fishermen of the gulf of Naples there was no difference apart from the locale, the language, and the work. The field and the waves inspire men with the same thoughts, whether they work on land or water. Nature speaks the same language to those who live with her, whether on the mountain or the sea.

We experienced the truth of all of this. Amid simple people, we found ourselves not outsiders but at home. The same instincts are like a common parent to all of us. The very monotony of this life pleased and quieted us. But we watched uneasily the end of summer and the days of autumn and winter approaching, which would require us to return to our own country. Our families were concerned and had begun asking us to return. We put off the idea of departure as much as we could, and we enjoyed pretending that this life we were living would go on forever.

VII

But September did come, with its rains and its thunderstorms. The sea turned less gentle. Our work grew harder and sometimes more dangerous. The winds grew colder, the whitecaps rose up and soaked us often with spray. On the pier, we had purchased two of those brown, rough woolen cloaks that the *lazzaroni* and the sailors of Naples throw over their shoulders during the winters. The wide sleeves of those cloaks hang down leaving the bare arms exposed. The hood, hanging behind or pulled up over the forehead depending on the weather, can either protect the mariner's head from rain or cold or allow the breezes to play through his dampened hair.

One day we left Margellina on a sea of glass, no breeze even so much as wrinkling the surface, to go fish for red mullets and the first tuna off the coast of Cumae, where the currents took them in that season. The thick morning fog hung in the air, and that meant the wind would be up in the evening. We hoped to avoid that and to have enough time to pass back by Miseno before the heavy, sleeping sea would be awakened.

The fish were plentiful. We wanted to throw out the nets a few more times. But the wind surprised us, blowing down from the heights of Mount Epomeo, the immense mountain that dominates the island of Ischia, and it seemed as if it were the sound and power of the mountain itself that came crashing down into the sea. First it flattened the water all around us, like an iron harrow flattening out the furrows in a field. And now the waves, recovering from the shock, swelled up loud and hollow, and within a few minutes they had risen to such a height that we were cut off from the sight of the coast and the islands.

We were equally distant now from both the coast and from Ischia, and we were already halfway through the canal that separates the Miseno cape from the Greek island of Procida. There was only one thing to do: row vigorously into the canal and if we succeeded in getting through, push ourselves off to the left, into the gulf of Baiae and take shelter there in its calmer waters.

The old fisherman never hesitated. From the top of a wave, where our boat was balanced for a moment amid a whirlpool of foam, he cast a quick glance around him, like a man who has lost his way and climbs up a tree to try to see his road. Then seizing hold of the rudder, he cried out: "To the oars, boys! We need to beat the wind to the cape; if it gets there first, we're done for!"

We obeyed him the way the body obeys an instinct.

Our eyes fixed on his to follow the rapid shifts in direction, we bent over our oars, and now painfully climbing the flank of a mounting wave, now hurtling down another along with its foam, we tried to control our ascent or descent by making use of the resistance of our oars in the water. Eight or ten waves, each more enormous than the last, hurled us through the narrowest part of the canal. But the wind had beaten us to the cape, as our pilot feared, and plunging between the cape and the tip of the island it had acquired such force that it was raising the sea up, seething and churning furiously, and the waves now finding no space to flee before the tempest that pursued them, rose up and redoubled in size, falling and crashing and spreading out in all directions as if the sea had gone mad and, trying to flee but unable to exit the canal, hurled themselves with terrible force against the steep rocks of the Miseno cape, raising up there a huge column of foam whose spray blew so far that it almost reached us.

VIII

Trying to get through that narrow passage with so fragile a boat, which could be filled and overwhelmed by a single wave, was madness. The fisherman looked over at the cape, visible by the enormous column of foam there, and his expression was one I will never forget. He made the sign of the cross and cried out to us, "Crossing is impossible, and getting back to the open sea is even worse. We have only one chance: get to Procida or drown."

Novices though we were in the ways of the sea, we could sense the difficulty of trying to get there during this storm. The wind was directing us toward the cape, pushing us ahead from our stern; we followed the sea, which seemed to be fleeing along with us, and the waves would hurl us up to their summits, so that we found ourselves rising and falling along with them. They had, therefore, less of a chance of sinking us into their abysses. But in order to make land at Procida—whose evening lights we could see off to our right—we would have to approach the waves obliquely and make our way along the valleys between them, in the direction of the coastline, keeping the thin boards of our boat's sides toward the waves and the wind. There was no time to hesitate. The fisherman signed for us to pick up our oars and took advantage of an interval between waves to get us turned in the right direction. We made our way toward Procida, riding the waves like a bit of seaweed tossed from wave to wave, one crest catching us from another one.

IX

We made slow progress; night fell. The spray, the foam, the torn and tattered clouds that the wind was blowing over the canal all made the night even darker. The old man had ordered the boy to light one of his resin torches in case it could either help give a little light to our maneuvers on the sea or perhaps be seen on Procida, letting people there know that a boat was in serious trouble in the canal, and asking them not for their help but for their prayers.

It was a sublime and an ominous spectacle, seeing that poor boy, with one hand gripping the little mast rising up out of the prow and with the other holding up above his head that fiery red torch, its flame being twisted and blown by the winds, searing his hands and burning his hair. That floating spark, appearing at the height of a wave and disappearing down its depths, always about to go out and always being reignited, was like a symbol of the four lives in the boat fighting for survival, hovering between salvation and death in the darkness and the anguish of that night.

X

Three hours passed thus, each minute of which stretched out to match our anxious thoughts. The moon rose and, as usually happens, the wind grew more furious as it did. If we had had the smallest sail still raised, we would have been capsized twenty times over. Although the boat's low sides meant that little of it was exposed to the tempestuous winds, there were still moments when we seemed to have been lifted right up off the waves, moments when it spun us around like a dry leaf blown from a tree.

We had taken on a great deal of water: we could not bail it out faster than it was coming in. There were moments when we felt the boards sinking down beneath us, like a coffin lowering into a grave. The weight of the water made the boat less obedient and made it harder to manage it between two waves. One second too slow, and everything would be lost.

The old man, unable to speak, made signals to us, with tears in his eyes, to throw everything we had overboard. The jars of water, the baskets filled with fish, the two thick sails, the iron anchor, the ropes, right down to the clothes, including our rough woolen cloaks, drenched and heavy now—all of it went over the side and into the sea. The poor helmsman watched all his wealth for a moment as it sank in the waters. The boat righted itself and now could ascend the crests of the waves like a horse that has dropped its burden.

We made our way insensibly into a quieter sea, sheltered a little by the western cape of Procida. The wind died down, the flame of the torch strengthened, and the moon opened up a great blue seam between the clouds; the waves stretched out and leveled off, ceasing to send their foam up over us. Bit by bit the sea grew shallower and began to lap around us as in a nearly quiet bay, and the black outline of the Procida shoreline was visible against the horizon. We were in the waters near the middle of the island's coast.

XI

But the sea was still too rough at this point to try to reach the port. We would have to approach the land from the side, coming in amid its reefs.

"Don't be worried anymore, boys," the fisherman said, seeing the coast by the light of the torch. "The Madonna has saved us. We'll get to shore and we'll sleep tonight in my house." We thought he must have lost his mind, because we didn't know that he had any house apart from the dark cellar in Margellina, and in order to get there that night, we would have to go back through the canal, pass the cape again, and once again confront the violent sea that we had only just escaped.

But he just smiled at our air of astonishment, as he could tell from our expressions what we had been thinking. "Rest assured, young people," he continued. "We'll get there without so much as having to fight one more wave."

He went on to explain that he was from Procida, and that he still owned a cabin and garden near the shore that had belonged to his father, and that at this very moment his aged wife and his granddaughter, sister to our ship boy Beppino, were in the house, drying figs and gathering grapes to sell in Naples.

"A few more strokes of the oar," he added, "and we'll be drinking fresh spring water, and that's clearer than the wines of Ischia."

We took heart at those words, and we rowed about the distance of a league along the coast of Procida, with its foaming waves. From time to time the boy would stand up and brandish the torch. It cast a sinister light on the rocks and illuminated a high wall of stone—nowhere to land. But at last, as we rounded a huge rampart of granite projecting out into the sea, we could see the cliff bending inward and hollowing out a little, like a breach in a castle wall; a quick turn of the rudder pointed us in, and our last three oar strokes pushed the harassed boat up between two rocks, the seafoam bubbling up on the shore.

XII

As the prow touched the rocks, it made a dry, sharp, cracking sound like a board being broken. We leaped out into the water and did the best we could to get the boat moored, using what was left of the ropes. We followed the old man and the child as they walked ashore ahead of us.

We climbed up the side of the cliff by means of a kind of narrow walkway that had been chiseled out of the rock; the steps were uneven, and they glistened with spray from the sea. The steep stairs up the rock face, which sometimes had missing steps, were soon followed by some artificial steps that had been formed by driving the points of long poles into holes in the rock, and then setting down either tarred planks from old boats on top of them or clumps of dead chestnut tree branches, their dried leaves still attached.

After we had slowly climbed up some four or five hundred such steps, we found ourselves in a small space surrounded by walls of gray stone. Toward the back of this space, two dark archways opened up, looking as if they were entryways to a storeroom. Above those two massive arches were two low, rounded, window-like openings, and above them rose a flat terraced roof, whose railings were decorated with flowerpots of rosemary and basil. Just below the windows we could make out a rough walkway, and in the bright moonlight we could see glistening bunches of maize suspended over it.

A door consisting of badly joined boards opened up on our space. To the right, the terrain upon which the little house was uneasily perched rose up to the level of the walkway. The branches of a large fig tree and some twisted vine stalks hung over one corner of the house, their leaves and fruits mingling together below the walkway, throwing off two or three serpentine shoots across the wall with the windows. Their branches formed a kind of grill over the two low windows opening up on that garden-like space; in fact, if it hadn't been for those windows, one might have taken the heavy, square, low house for another one of the great gray rocks on this coastline, or for one of those solidified blocks of lava that the chestnut, ivy, and vines embraced and buried beneath their branches—those great lava blocks that the wine-growers of Castellammare or Sorrento hollow out and then install a door over the opening, using the interior as a place for storing their wine close to the vines that gave birth to it.

Out of breath from our long, steep, rapid climb and weighted down by the oars we still carried on our shoulders, we stopped still a moment, we and the old man, to catch our breath in this open space. But the boy, throwing his oar down on top of a heap of underbrush and scampering quickly up the stairway, began to knock on one of the windows with his lit torch in one hand, calling out joyfully to his grandmother and sister: "Grandma! Sister! *Madre! Sorellina!*" He cried out, "Gaetana! Graziella! Wake up! Open up; it's father and me; we have strangers with us."

We heard a sleepy voice, but a clear, gentle one, calling out confusedly some exclamations of surprise from inside the house. Then the panel of one of the windows opened up halfway, pushed outward by a bare, white arm that stretched out from a loose, flowing sleeve. We could see by the gleam of the torch that the boy held up toward the window the ravishing shape of a young girl appearing on tiptoe between the open shutters.

Surprised in the middle of the night by the voice of

her brother, Graziella had not had time to think of covering herself more fully before opening the window. She had hurried barefoot toward the window dressed just as she had been in her bed. Half of her long black hair hung down over one side of her face, while the other half curled around her neck or, lifted by the wind that was blowing forcefully, flapped against the half-opened shutter and then returned to whip against her face, like the wing of a raven battling against the wind.

She rubbed her eyes with the backs of her hands, raising her elbows and stretching out her shoulders with that gesture of the child who has been awakened and wants only to go back to sleep. Her nightshirt, tied around her neck, revealed only the outlines of her tall, slim torso; the thin cloth just covered the first undulations of youthful flesh. Her eyes, oval and large, were of that indistinct shade between a deep black and the blue of the sea, a shade that softens the eyes' radiance by a certain warmth in a woman's gaze, uniting the sweetness of her soul with the power of her passions—a celestial tint that the women of both Asia Minor and Italy borrow equally from the burning suns and the serene, azure skies under which they live, and from the azure of their sea and the azure of their night. Her cheeks were full, round, firm, naturally a little pale, but darkened a bit by the climate—not that sickly pallor of the North but that healthful whiteness of the South that reminds one of marble that has been exposed to the air and sea for centuries. Her lips were open and a little thinner than those of the women of our climate, and her mouth was marked at the corners by those small wrinkles that suggest candor and good nature. Her teeth were small but strikingly white, reflecting the light of the torch like pearls by the coastline, shimmering beneath the sun-streaked water.

While she spoke to her younger brother, her words, a little sharp and emphatic, were half-carried off by the wind, but they nevertheless sounded like music to us. Her facial expressions, as mobile as the shifting gleams of the torch that illuminated her, swiftly changed from surprise to fear, from fear to gaiety, from gentle concern to laughter; then she caught sight of us by the trunk of the great fig tree, and she retreated in confusion from the window, her hand abandoning the shutter that now freely banged against the wall; she hurriedly awoke her grandmother and got herself half-dressed and then came to open the door to us, embracing her grandfather and brother with emotion.

XIII

The old woman soon appeared, holding up a red earthenware lantern that illuminated her thin, pale face and her hair, white as the skein of wool that lay heaped on the table like snow. She kissed her husband's hand and the boy's forehead. The entire story related here was told in just a few words and gestures among the members of the poor family. We couldn't understand all of it. We kept off to one side so as not to interfere in our hosts' pouring out their hearts to each other. They were poor; we were foreigners, strangers; we owed them our respect. We stood aside, near the door, watching them in silence.

Graziella cast a glance our way from time to time, seeming surprised to see us there, as if she were half in a dream. When the grandfather finished telling the story, the old woman went down on her knees by the hearth, and Graziella climbed upon the terrace, bringing back a rosemary branch and some orange blossoms, like big white stars. Using long pins she took from her hair, she fashioned them into a bouquet and, standing on a chair, fastened it under a little statue of the Virgin that stood above the doorway; a lamp burned before it, rendering the statue a smoky color. We understood that all this was an act of thanksgiving to their divine protectress for having saved her grandfather and her brother; we paid our respects as well.

XIV

The house was as bare inside as the rocks outside, and the interior resembled them too. The walls were unplastered, whitened only by a coat of lime. Lizards, awakened by the light, slithered and rustled in the crevices between the rocks and beneath the fern leaves that served as beds for the children. Nests, from which the tiny heads of swallows peeped out, their eyes uneasily glittering in the light, were hung from the beams, still covered with bark, which formed the roof. Graziella and her grandmother slept together in the second room, on a single bed covered with scraps of linen. The floor was strewn with baskets for fruits and a mule saddle.

The fisherman turned to us with an embarrassed air, gesturing to indicate the poverty of his home; then he led us out onto the terrace, which is a place of honor in the Orient and the south of Italy.[19] With help from the boy and Graziella, he fashioned a sort of lean-to for us by propping the end of one of the oars against the wall of the parapet and the other end against the floor. He made a roof out of a dozen branches from a chestnut tree, which had been recently cut on the mountain; he laid several sheaves of fern leaves on the ground; and he then brought us two pieces of bread, some fresh water, and some figs, inviting us to sleep there.

The fatigue and the emotions of the day soon had us in a deep sleep. When we awoke, the swallows were already chirping around our bed and scouring the terrace for any crumbs left over from our supper, and the sun, already high in the sky, like a furnace was heating the branches that served as our roof.

We lay a long time stretched out on our bed of ferns, in that state of half-sleep that allows the mental side of the man to observe and think before the physical side has the courage to get up and move about. We exchanged a few inarticulate words now and then, interrupting the long silences from which we fell back into dreaming. The previous day's fishing, the boat rocking beneath our feet, the furious sea, the inaccessible rocks on the shore, the face of Graziella gazing out from between the shutters: all these images spun and intermixed, becoming a confused whole within our dreams.

We were pulled up and out of that somnolence by hearing the sobs and reproaches of the old grandmother, who was talking to her husband in the house. The chimney, which had an opening on the terrace side, carried the voices and some of the words out to us. The poor woman was lamenting the loss of the jars, the anchor, the almost-new ropes, and above all the two fine sails woven with hemp by her own hands, which we had been barbaric enough to hurl into the sea in order to save our lives.

"What business did you have," she was saying to the dismayed and mute old man, "in picking up two strangers, these two Frenchmen you brought home? Don't you know that they're pagans [*pagani*] and that they bring bad luck and impiety with them? The saints punished you. They've taken away our wealth, and now the one thing you'd better do is thank them for not taking away our souls as well."

The poor man didn't know how to respond. But Graziella, with the authority and the patience of a child whose grandmother forbids her nothing, objected to the injustice of her reproaches, and she took the old man's part:

"What do you mean, these strangers are pagans?" she asked her grandmother. "Do pagans show the kind of compassion they showed for poor people? Do pagans make the sign of the cross like we do before a holy image? Well, I can tell you that yesterday while you were on your knees thanking God, when I fixed the bouquet next to the image of the Madonna, I saw them both bow their heads as if they were praying and make the sign of the cross on their chests, and I even saw a tear in the eye of the younger one; I saw it drop onto his hand."

"That was just a drop of seawater dripping off his hair," the old woman interjected acidly.

"No, I tell you it was a tear," Graziella insisted with some heat. "The wind was blowing strong enough to dry their hair between leaving the coast and arriving up here on the summit. But the wind doesn't dry up the heart. And I'll say it again: there was water in their eyes." We understood that we had a protectress, one who was all-powerful in that house, because the grandmother said nothing in reply and ceased her muttering.

XV

We hurried down from the terrace to thank the poor family for the hospitality they showed us. We found the fisherman, the old woman, Beppo, Graziella, and even the little ones getting ready to go down to the shore to examine the boat abandoned the night before, to see if it was well enough moored in the bad weather, for the storm had still not stopped. We descended with them, our faces downcast and timid like guests who have been the cause of some trouble in a family and who are not quite sure how the family feels about them.

The fisherman and his wife went a few steps ahead of the rest; Graziella, holding one of her little brothers by the hand and carrying the other in her arms, came next, and we followed behind, in silence. At the last turning of one of the sets of steps, we could see the shoals that had previously been obscured by the rocks, and as the group approached the spot we heard both the fisherman and his wife emit a shriek of horror. We saw them lifting their bare arms up toward the sky, twisting their hands as if in the convulsions of despair, beating their foreheads, and tearing out tufts of their white hair, which the wind carried away, twisting in the air, floating down toward the rocks below.

Graziella and the little ones joined in the wailing as well. Everyone rushed down the final steps as if they were mad, racing toward the shoals, running practically into the foam being hurled onto the shore by the immense waves; some were on their knees, some prostrated themselves; the old woman lay in the damp sand, covering her face with her hands.

We contemplated this scene of despair from the height of the stairway's last landing, unable either to move forward or go back. The boat, moored to the rock but with no anchor to hold it in place, had been upended during the night by the waves and had been shattered into pieces on the sharp points of the rocks that should have protected it. Half of the old skiff remained roped to the rock where we had left it the night before. It made a sinister scraping sound as it beat against the rock, like the hoarse groan of damned souls.

The other parts of the hull, the stern, the mast, the ribs, the painted seats—all were scattered here and there on the beach, looking like parts of bodies that had been ripped up by wolves after a battle. When we got down onto the beach, the old fisherman was busy rushing from one piece of debris to another. He picked them up, looked them over with a cold eye, then let them fall at his feet and moved on. Graziella sat on the ground and wept, her face in her apron. The children, their limbs bare, were crying out as they raced around in the water trying to nudge floating pieces of the boat toward the shore.

The old woman never ceased wailing, and she never ceased talking as she wailed. We could only make out bits and pieces of what she said, as the wind took her lamentations and dispersed them in the air, but what we could hear touched our hearts. "O, ferocious sea! Deaf sea! Sea worse than the demons of hell! Heartless sea, shameless sea!" She exclaimed phrases like these along with curses, shaking her fists at the waves. "Why didn't you take us too? All of us? Since you've taken away our means of living! Oh come, come and take pieces of me, if you won't take all of me!"

And saying this she rose up and seated herself, tearing at the rags of her dress and throwing tufts of her hair into the sea. She shook her fist at the sea, and standing up she kicked at the foam at her feet; then, passing back and forth between rage and lament, convulsions and grief, she sat back down on the sand, putting her face in her hands and weeping as she gazed on the scattered planks beating against the rocks. "Poor boat!" she cried, as if the pieces of wood were the members of some beloved one who had just passed on. "Is this the end you deserved? Shouldn't we have perished with you? Perish together, just as we have lived together? Look at you, lying here in pieces and shreds, in the dirt, crying out all night long while we should have heard and come to help you! What must you think of us! You have served us so well, and we have betrayed you, abandoned you, lost you! Lost, lost, and so close to the house, so close to the voice of your master! Thrown on the shore like the corpse of a faithful dog rejected by the waves, thrown back at the feet of the master who drowned it!"

Her voice was stifled by tears for a moment, but then she began to enumerate, one by one, all the qualities of their boat, and all the money it had cost them, and all the memories she attached to that poor pile of floating debris. "Was it for this," she said, "that we worked so hard to refit and repaint it after the last tuna season? And was it for this that my poor son, before he died and left me with his three children, fatherless and motherless, built it with so much care and so much love—built it almost entirely with his own two hands? When I would come to take the baskets of fish out of the hold, I would recognize his hatchet marks on the wood, and I would kiss them in memory of him. The sharks and the sea crabs will kiss them now! During winter evenings, he used his knife to carve the image of St. Francis on a board, and he fixed it on the prow for protection against bad weather.[20] Oh, you pitiless saint! How have you shown your gratitude? What have you done with my son, with his wife, and with the boat he left behind for us to earn a living and feed his poor children? How have you protected yourself—and where is your image now, the plaything of the waves?"

"Mother! Mother!" cried one of the children on the beach, pulling out from between two rocks a piece of board left behind by the waves. "Here's the saint!" The poor woman immediately forgot all her rage and all her blasphemies, rushing through the water to get to the child, and she picked up the piece of wood carved by her son, pressing her lips to it and covering it with her tears. Then she sat down on the shore and said no more.

XVI

We helped Beppo and the old man retrieve, one by one, all the pieces of the boat. We dragged the mutilated keel farther up onto the beach. We made a pile of the debris, some boards and hinges of which could still be of some use to the poor family; we rolled some heavy rocks on top of the heap, so that the waves, if they came up that far, would not further disperse these revered remains of the skiff; and then we climbed back up, sad and far behind our hosts, to the house. The absence of a boat as well as the state of the sea meant there was no way we could depart.

Later, our eyes lowered and without saying a word, we accepted a piece of bread and some goat's milk that Graziella brought to us near the fountain, beneath the fig tree, and we then left the house to its mourning and went off to walk beneath the high vine arbor and the olive trees growing on the island's plateau.

XVII

We spoke very little, my friend and I, but our thoughts were the same, and we instinctively took the pathways that led to the eastern side of the island, toward the town of Procida. We encountered a few goatherds and some girls in Greek dress carrying jars of oil balanced on their heads, and they all assured us we were on the right path. After about an hour's walk, we finally arrived at the town.

My friend said after a while, "Well, this was a sad enough adventure."

"We have to make it up to those good people some-how," I said.

"I've been thinking about that," he said, tapping his finger on his belt and rattling the coins inside.

"Me too, but I have only five or six sequins in my wallet. I had an equal share in the catastrophe, so I should have an equal share in the reparations."

"I'm the richer of the two of us," said my friend. "I have credit with a banker in Naples. I can advance the whole amount, and we can settle up our accounts when we get back to France."

XVIII

Conversing in this way, we slowly descended the hilly streets into Procida. We soon came to the *marine*. The beach was covered with boats from Ischia, Procida, and Naples that the previous day's storm had forced into safe harbor. Some sailors and fishermen dozed in the sun to the sounds of the gradually decreasing waves, while others sat in groups on the piers and chatted. With the clothes we were wearing and our red woolen caps, they took us for young sailors from Tuscany or Genoa who had come here on one of the ships carrying oil or Ischian wine.

We roamed around the *marine* looking for a solid and well-rigged boat that could be easily maneuvered by two men, one whose size and shape were as close as possible to the one that had been wrecked the night before. It wasn't hard to find one. It belonged to a rich fisherman of the island, a man who owned a number of other boats. This one had only seen a few months of service. We went to the proprietor's house, our way there guided by children from the port.

He was a cheery, sensible, decent sort. He seemed touched by the story we told about the night's disaster and the desolation of his poor Procida compatriot. He made sure that he did not lose a single piaster on the price of the boat, but he did not exaggerate its value either, and we reached an agreement to buy the boat for thirty-two golden sequins, which my friend paid him on the spot. The sum being paid, the boat and its brand-new rigging—sails, water jars, ropes, an iron anchor—all belonged to us.

We completed our equipment in a harbor shop by purchasing two brown woolen cloaks, one for the old man and one for the boy; we also bought some diverse kinds of nets, some baskets for fish, and some larger household utensils for the women to use. We told the man selling the boat that we would pay him an additional three sequins the next day if the boat could be readied and taken that same day to a particular spot on the coastline. Since the storm was abating and the elevation of the island tended to lessen the wind on that area of the shore, he agreed, and we took our way back, walking overland, to the house of Andrea.

XIX

We walked along slowly, sitting down from time to time beneath the trees or in the shade of the trellises, chatting, dreaming, haggling with all the young Procidans who wanted to sell us the figs, medlar fruits, and grapes they carried in baskets, and simply letting time pass. When from the height of a promontory we were able to see our new boat furtively slipping out under the shadow of the coastline, we increased our pace in order to arrive at the same time as the rowers.

Not a sound could be heard from the little house and the vines that surrounded it. Two fine pigeons with white wings streaked with black were pecking at little bits of corn on the floor of the terrace, the sole sign of any life in the house. We went up on the roof silently, and there we found the entire family in a deep sleep. All of them, except the two little ones who slept in Graziella's arms, their pretty heads resting side by side, were asleep in the posture of exhaustion that comes from too much sorrow.

The old woman's head rested on her knees, and her heavy breathing still sounded like sobs. The man was stretched out on his back, his arms crossed, in the bright sunlight. The little swallows grazed his hair as they flitted past. There were flies on his sweating face. Two deep furrows wound down his face to his mouth, testifying that the man's strength had been broken and that he had fallen asleep weeping.

The sight touched us to the core, but the thought of the happiness we were about to bring to them consoled us. We woke them up, tossing down toward the feet of Graziella and her little brothers, right onto the floor, the fresh bread, cheese, salted meat, grapes, oranges, and figs that we had bought on our way back. The girl and the little ones hardly dared stand up for the abundance that seemed to come out of the heavens and was raining down on them. The father thanked us for his family, but the grandmother looked upon the scene with no expression, though her face communicated anger rather than indifference.

"Come, Andrea," my friend said to the old man, "a man should not weep twice for something he can replace with some work and some courage. Planks can be hewn from the forest, and sails can be made from hemp. The only thing that can't be replaced is the life of a man when it's worn out by grieving. One day of weeping takes more out of us than a year of working. Come down with us, with your wife and the children. We'll be your sailors; we will help you carry all the debris from your shipwreck up here. You can use it to make fencing, beds, tables, furniture for your family. In your old age someday, it will be a pleasure for you to sleep peacefully among those planks, the ones that had borne you so long on the waves."

"May they be used for our coffins," muttered the grandmother.

XX

Nonetheless, they all got up and followed us in our slow descent to the shore, but it was evident that the sight of the sea and the sound of the waves disturbed them. I will not try to describe the surprise and the joy of these poor people when, from the height of the last landing on the stairway, they caught sight of the new boat, gleaming in the sun, hauled up on the sand next to the debris of the old one. When my friend announced, "She is yours!" they fell to their knees as if thunderstruck, each one on the stair step where they stood, and thanked God before finding the words to thank us. But their happiness was all the thanks we needed.

They stood up when they heard my friend calling to them, and they all ran down toward the boat. They first made a slow, careful, and respectful tour of it, as if they were afraid that it was only some kind of mirage or that it would suddenly vanish like a magic trick. Then they slowly drew closer, then touched it, and then brought the hands that had touched it up to their foreheads and to their lips. Finally they broke out in exclamations of wonder and joy, and clasping hands together, they all, from the old woman to the little ones, formed a chain and danced around the boat.

XXI

Beppo was the first one to climb in. Standing up on the little deck in the prow, he pulled out from the hold, one by one, all the equipment we had stocked in it: the anchor, the ropes, the four-handled water jars, the fine new canvas, the baskets, the cloaks with their wide sleeves; he made the anchor ring, raised the oars up over his head, unfurled the sail, rubbed the rough cloth of the cloaks between his fingers, and displayed all these riches to his grandfather, to his grandmother, to his sister, all while shouting and hopping up and down with glee. The father, the mother, and Graziella all wept as their gaze moved back and forth, again and again, between the boat and us.

The sailors who had delivered the boat, hiding behind the rocks, wept too. Everyone heaped blessings upon us. Graziella, her face lowered and with the greatest seriousness, approached her grandmother and, pointing toward us, said, "You called them pagans, and I said that they might be angels. Now which one of us was right?"

The old woman knelt down before us and begged our pardon for her suspicions. From that hour on, she loved us almost as much as she loved her granddaughter or her Beppo.

XXII

We dismissed the Procida sailors after paying them the agreed-upon three sequins. We all took one of the objects from the boat's hold and carried it up to the house; instead of carrying up pieces of debris, we carried up the new wealth of the happy family. That evening after supper, by the light of the lamp, Beppo detached from his grandmother's bed the broken piece of plank bearing the likeness of St. Francis that had been carved by his father; he squared it with a saw and scraped it clean with his knife; he polished and repainted it. He proposed affixing it to the inside of the new boat's prow in the morning, so that there would be something of the old boat inside the new. In the same way, the peoples of antiquity, when they erected a temple atop the ruins of an old one, took care to include some element of the old one, whether some building materials or a given column or the like, so that something of the old and the sacred would be included in the modern, and so that the memory itself, even if crude and worn, would retain its worship and its sway over the heart even among the masterpieces of the new sanctuary. Man is always and everywhere man. His nature always follows the same instincts, whether it is a matter of the Parthenon, of

St. Peter's in Rome, or of a poor fisherman's boat on a reef on Procida.

XXIII

That night may have been the happiest of all the nights Providence had destined for the house, from the time it had been hewn out of the rock all the way to the time when it would crumble back into dust. We slept with the wind blowing through the olive trees, with the waves breaking against the coast, and with the moon casting its light down on our terrace. When we awoke, the sky had been swept as clean as polished crystal, and the sea was darkened and streaked with foam as if it had been sweating from its efforts and its fatigue. But the wind, even more furious now, continued its howling. The white spray that the waves tossed up at the point of Cape Miseno rose up even higher than it had the day before. It was bathing the coast of Cumae in the ebb and flow of a luminous fog that never ceased rising up and falling back down. No sails were visible on the gulf of Gaeta or on that of Baia. The sea swallows whipped the foam with their white wings, the only birds that find their element within the tempest and that call out with joy during shipwrecks, like the accursed inhabitants of the Bay of the Dead, who prey on lost ships.[21]

We felt, without having to say it, a secret joy at being imprisoned by the weather in the old fisherman's house and vineyard. It gave us the time to savor our situation and to share in the happiness of the poor family, to whom we were becoming attached, like children.

The wind and the high seas kept us there for nine whole days. We both would have liked—I especially would have liked—for the storm to go on forever and for us to be forced to stay there, letting the years pass by in this place where we found ourselves so fortunately trapped. Our nine days, though, passed by insensibly, each one like the others. There is no better proof for how few things are necessary for happiness when the heart is young and takes pleasure in everything. Likewise, the simplest foods will sustain and rejuvenate the body when the appetite seasons them and when the organs are young and healthy . . .

XXIV

Awaking to the cry of the swallows fluttering around the leafy roof of the terrace where we were sleeping; hearing the childlike voice of Graziella, singing softly to herself among the vines for fear of waking up the two foreigners; descending swiftly down to the beach to plunge ourselves into the sea and swim for a few minutes in a small inlet where the fine sand glitters within the transparency of the deep water, an inlet where the high waves of the sea never penetrate; climbing back up to the house slowly while toweling off, the sun warming and drying our hair and shoulders; eating, in the vineyard, a piece of bread with some buffalo milk cheese, brought to us and shared with us by the young lady herself; drinking the clear, fresh spring water, carried by her in the little oblong earthenware jar, which she tilted toward our lips by balancing it on her arm, blushing as she did so; then helping the family with the thousand little rustic tasks around the house and garden: shoring up the wall that surrounds the vineyard and supports the terraces; picking up big stones that had rolled down during the winter onto the young vine plants, reducing the space available for planting; carrying down into the cellar the great yellow gourds, so big that only one can be carried at a time; then trimming back the vines whose broad leaves cover the ground and whose busy networks make walking difficult; digging a shallow ditch between each row of vines, under the high trellises, so that the rainwater will pool up and keep the plants watered longer; digging, for the very same purpose, a kind of well at the foot of the fig and lemon trees: such were our morning occupations, up until the hour when the sun shot its rays right down on the roof, on the garden, on the courtyard, forcing us to find shelter in the shade of the trellises. The sun shone through and reflected off of the vine leaves, tinting the wavering shadows a warm, almost golden color.

I

Graziella would then go back inside the house to sew beside her grandmother or prepare the midday meal. The old fisherman and Beppo would spend whole days by the seaside preparing the new boat, working on all the ideas for little perfections that their new property inspired in them, and testing out their nets in the safe waters of the inlet. Often they would bring up to us for our midday meal some crabs or some eels, whose skins glistened like just-fired lead. The old woman would fry them up in olive oil. The family kept this oil, as was the custom of the region, in a little well drilled into the rock close to the house and capped with a heavy stone fitted with an iron ring. Some cucumbers cut into strips and fried on the stove, some fresh shellfish similar to mussels, which they called *frutti di mare*, comprised our frugal dinner, the principal and the most succulent one of the day. Dessert was muscatel grapes in long, yellow bunches still on their stems and still with their leaves, picked by Graziella that same morning and served on wicker basket plates. A stalk or two of green, raw fennel dipped in pepper, the anise-like scent of which freshens the breath and warms the heart, was our substitute for liqueurs and coffee, as was the custom among the sailors and peasants of Naples. After dinner my friend and I would go in search of some cool, shaded retreat up on the summit of the cliff, from which we could see the bay and the coast of Baia; we would pass the hottest hours of the day there, watching, dreaming, and reading until four or five hours after noon.

II

We had only been able to preserve from the waves three mismatched volumes, for they happened not to have been in the sailors' valise we threw into the ocean that night: first was a thin Italian volume by Ugo Foscolo titled *Letters of Jacopo Ortis*, a kind of *Werther*, half-politics and half-romance, in which a young Italian's passion for the liberty of his native land melds with his passion for a beautiful Venetian.[1] This double enthusiasm, nourished by the double intensities of lover and patriot, ignites in the soul of Ortis a kind of fever that proves to be too strong for a sensitive and delicate man and leads him ultimately to suicide. This book, too closely copied from Goethe's *Werther* but nonetheless nuanced and luminous, was at the time being read by all the young men who, like us, were nourishing within their souls that double dream of those who are worthy of having truly grand dreams: both love and liberty.

III

The police of Bonaparte and Murat had banned the author and book, but in vain. The author found his sanctuary in the hearts of all Italian patriots and those of all the liberals across Europe. The book found its home and its refuge in the hearts of young people like us; we hid it away there so that we could breathe in its maxims. As to the other two volumes we had saved, one was *Paul et Virginie* by Bernardin de Saint-Pierre, that manual of innocent love; the book seems like a page from the childhood of the world torn from the history of the human heart and conserved, entirely pure and steeped in the contagious tears of sixteen-year-olds.[2]

The third was a volume of Tacitus, its pages soiled by tales of debauchery, of shame and blood, but pages wherein stoic virtue takes up the chisel and sculpts from impassible history an inspiration for readers from future ages, transmitting to them a hatred of tyranny, a reverence for great devotion, and the desire for a noble death.[3]

These three books, though surviving by chance, corresponded to the three feelings that caused our young hearts to vibrate: love, an enthusiasm for the liberation of Italy and of France, and finally, a passion for political action and for the upheaval of great events, the image of which we saw in Tacitus; his brush was steeped in blood, and he steeped our hearts in it too, communicating to us the power of ancient heroism. We read him out loud, taking turns, sometimes marveling, sometimes weeping, sometimes dreaming. Our readings were punctuated by long silences and mutual exclamations, which formed a running, spontaneous commentary of our impressions—a commentary carried off by the wind, along with our dreams.

IV

We would imagine ourselves in one of the fictional or real situations that the poet or historian had just narrated to us. We would fashion ourselves into the ideal lover or the ideal patriot, living a hidden life or a public one, one of happiness or one of virtue. We would amuse ourselves by combining great events and marvelous situations from eras of revolution, the kind of moments where entirely unknown men step forward out of the crowd by virtue of their genius and are called—truly called, as if a voice had called out their own names—to combat tyranny and save nations; later, victims of instability and the ingratitude of the people, they are condemned to die on the scaffold, misunderstood by their historical moment but avenged by posterity.

There could have been no role, no matter how heroic, that we would not have risen to, given the situation. We were prepared for anything, and if fate failed to present us with the grand circumstances we imagined, we would avenge ourselves by our contempt for fate. We felt the consolation that strong hearts always feel: that if our lives ended up unimportant, vulgar, and obscure, it was destiny that had failed us and not we who failed destiny!

V

When the sun sank, we took long excursions across the island. We covered it in every direction. We went to town to buy bread or the vegetables that Andrea's garden lacked. Sometimes we would bring some tobacco back with us, that opium of the sailor that animates him at sea and consoles him on land. We would return at nightfall, our pockets and hands filled with our little luxuries. The family would all come together then on the roof that in Naples is called the *astrico*, for the few hours before going to bed. Nothing is more picturesque in the fine nights of that climate than the scene on the *astrico* by the light of the moon.

Out in the country, the low, square house looks like an ancient pedestal supporting living groups, animated statues. All the house's inhabitants gather up on the roof, moving around or sitting down in various postures; the moonlight or the glow from the lamp projects and outlines their profiles against the blue firmament. You see the old woman sewing; the father smoking his pipe made of clay, its stem made of a reed; the children at the roof's edge leaning on their elbows, singing with prolonged notes those sea or farm songs, the accent and vibrato of which sound something like the way a wooden boat sounds on the waves, or something like the humming of the grasshopper in the sun; and you see the girls with their short dresses and bare feet, their green vests embroidered in gold or silk thread, their long black hair wafting over their shoulders, covered with the kerchief that they knot around their necks to protect their hair from the dust.

Often, they dance alone or with their sisters; one plays a guitar, while the other raises up over her head a tambourine with tiny brass cymbals. These two instruments, the one plaintive and nimble, the other monotone and heavy, fit together marvelously to render, almost artlessly, the two alternating notes of the human heart: sorrow and joy. You can hear them during summer nights on practically all the rooftops on the islands or the countryside around Naples, and even on the boats; this aerial concert, pursuing the ear as you move from site to site, from the sea to the mountains, sounds like the buzzing of some new insect, born from the heat and humming under that beautiful sky. And this poor insect is man! Man, who sings before God for a little while about his youth and loves and then is silent for all eternity. I have never been able to hear that sound spreading out through the air from the height of the *astricos* without stopping and feeling my heart tighten, ready either to burst out into an inner joy or to give way to a melancholy that is stronger than I am.

VI

Such were the postures, the music, and the voices on Andrea's roof terrace. Graziella played the guitar and Beppino accompanied his sister, making his child's fingers dance on the tambourine that, not long before, had helped lull him to sleep in his cradle. Cheerful as the instruments were, joyful as the attitudes were, the airs themselves were somehow sorrowful, as the slow, spare notes penetrated deeply and wrung the sleeping fibers of the heart. This is the way of music everywhere, so long as it is not reduced to a vain jingle for the ear but instead is allowed to express the harmonious yearnings of the passions, rising up out of the heart and into the voice. Then all its accents are sighs, all its notes afloat in tears of sound. Whenever the human heart is struck with even a little force, tears inevitably arise, so deeply is our nature steeped in sadness! And when it is shaken, how the sediment rises to our lips and the mists to our eyes!

VII

Even when we had successfully coaxed the young girl and she rose modestly to dance the tarantella for us, to the beat of the tambourine played by her brother, and when inspired by the wild motions of that national dance she whirled before us, her arms gracefully raised and imitating with her fingers the clacking of castanets, the quick steps of her bare feet pattering on the terrace like drops of rain—and yes, even in the air, in the postures, in the very frenzy of the delirious movement there was something serious, something sad, as if all human joys were only passing illusions, and as if in order to seize even a moment of happiness, youth and beauty themselves had to resort to the vertiginous intoxication of movement, even to the point of madness!

VIII

More often we would converse seriously with our hosts, getting them to tell us about their lives, their traditions, and their family memories. Every family is a history, and even a poem, for the one who knows how to read it. This one had had its nobility, its affluence, and its prestige in the long ago.

Andrea's grandfather had been a Greek merchant from the isle of Aegina. Persecuted for his religion by the ruling pasha at Athens, he set off one night with his wife, his daughters, his sons, and his entire fortune in one of the boats he used in his business. He took refuge in Procida, where he had had some clients and where the population was Greek, like him. He had bought up a great deal of property, of which the only thing remaining was the little farm where we were and the names of his ancestors engraved on some tombstones in the city's cemetery. The daughters had died as nuns in the island's convent. The sons had lost all the family fortune when some storms at sea destroyed their ships. The family fell into a state of decay and had changed its fine Greek name to that of an obscure fisherman in Procida. "When a house crumbles, eventually even the last stone gets swept away," Andrea told us. "Out of everything that my ancestors owned under the skies of heaven, all that now remains are my two oars, the boat you have returned to me, this house and garden, which cannot even support its owners, and the grace of God."

IX

The mother and the girl asked us to tell them, in turn, who we were, where we came from, what our families did; whether we had fathers, mothers, brothers or sisters, a house, fig trees and vines; and why we had left all that behind to come here to row, read, write, and daydream in the sun and sleep at night by the gulf of Naples. We were never able to make them understand that we had come to look at the sky and the sea, to let our souls dilate in the sun, to feel our youth ripen and grow within us, and to gather impressions, feelings, ideas that we might someday turn into poems, like those they saw us reading in our books, or like those that the improvisers of Naples recited on Sunday evenings to sailors on the quays or at Margellina.

"You're making fun of us," Graziella said, breaking out into a laugh. "You two as poets! But you don't have disheveled hair and haggard-looking eyes, like the ones they call by that name over on the quays. You two, poets! And you don't even know how to play a note on the guitar. How on earth are you going to accompany the songs you write?"

And she shook her head and made a face, becoming impatient with us when we insisted that we were telling the truth.

X

Sometimes a grim suspicion would occur to her, and her gaze would take on a shadow of doubt and fear when she looked at us. But this didn't last. And we heard her saying quietly to her grandmother, "No, it's not possible; they can't be refugees on the run from their country for some awful crime. They're too young and too good to know any such evil." After that, we amused ourselves by making up stories in which we had committed sinister crimes. But the contrast between our calm faces with our serene, limpid eyes, our smiling lips and our open hearts with the fantastical crimes we were supposed to have committed, ended up by making both her and her brother burst into laughter and quickly dissipated any possibility of distrust.

XI

Graziella asked us often what it was that we were reading all day long. She thought that the books must be books of prayers, for she had never seen books outside of the ones in the church, in the hands of the faithful who knew how to read and could follow along with the holy words spoken by the priest. She thought we must be quite pious, the way we would spend whole days muttering mysterious words. She was surprised that we were not going to become priests or hermits in a Naples seminary or some monastery on the islands. To explain it to her, we tried to read out loud to her, translating into the vulgate of her region, some passages from Foscolo and some fine pieces from our Tacitus.

We thought that those patriotic effusions from the exiled Italian and the great tragedies from imperial Rome would make a strong impression on our naive auditors, for their country is an instinctual matter for the people, and their feelings are naturally heroic, their gaze naturally dramatic. What really stay with them are stories about the falls of the great ones and fine deaths. But we quickly saw that the scenes that had been so powerful for us had no effect at all on these simple hearts. The passion for political liberty, which is always the aspiration of men of leisure, does not penetrate so deeply down into the people.

These poor fishermen could not comprehend why Ortis was in such despair and why he killed himself, since he could have enjoyed all the real pleasures in life: to walk along with nothing pressing that he had to do, to see the sun, to love his mistress, and to pray to God along the river Brenta, with its grassy banks. "Why torment yourself," they asked, "over ideas that have no connection to your heart? Who cares whether it's the Austrians or the French who reign in Milan? Only a fool would get so upset over things like that." And they turned and stopped listening.

XII

As for Tacitus, they were even less interested. Empire or republic, the men killing each other, some to reign and others to avoid servitude, all the crimes committed for the throne, all those virtues practiced for the sake of glory, all those deaths for the sake of posterity—it all left them cold. The grand storms of history played themselves out too far above their heads for them to be affected by them. For them, such things were like the thunder one hears up on the mountain, which can be ignored because it will only affect the heights and would not so much as fill the sail of the fisherman or ever touch the house of the farmer.

Tacitus is only popular among politicians and philosophers; he is the Plato of history. His sensibility is too refined for the common reader. To understand him, one must have lived among the tumults of public places or among the mysterious intrigues of the palace. Remove liberty, ambition, and glory from these scenes, and what remains? They are the three great actors of Tacitus's drama. And they are the three passions unknown to the common people, because they are passions of the mind and not of the heart. We could see this when we felt the coolness and the surprise that our fragments of stories elicited.

So one evening we tried reading to them from *Paul et Virginie*. It fell to me to translate while reading, because I had read the book so often that I had it more or less by heart. Our long stay in Italy had familiarized me with the language, so finding the right expressions came easily to me, and words rolled off my tongue as if I were speaking in my maternal language. My reading had barely begun when I saw the faces of my little audience begin to show interest and receptivity, a sure indicator that the heart has become involved. We had discovered the chord that pulses in unison with the heart in all people, in all ages, and in all social conditions, the sympathetic chord, the universal one, the one that contains within its single sound the eternal truth of art: nature, love, and God.

XIII

I had only read a few pages and already the old people, the girl, the child, all of them had changed their postures and attitudes. The fisherman, his elbow on his knee, his ear bent toward me, forgot to smoke his pipe. The old grandmother, sitting across from me, leaned her chin on her two hands in that gesture that poor women make when they are listening to the word of God, kneeling on the stone floors of temples. Beppo came down from the top of the terrace wall where he had been perching. He noiselessly laid his guitar down on the floor and carefully laid his hand across the strings, for fear that the wind would make them resonate. Graziella, who normally kept some distance between us, insensibly moved closer to me, as if she had been fascinated by the book's power of attraction.

Leaning herself up against the terrace wall, where I was sitting too, she moved closer and closer toward my side, leaning over on her left hand in the posture of the *Dying Gaul*.[4] Her wide-open eyes stared now at the book, now at my lips, from which the story was flowing, and sometimes at the gap between my lips and the book, as if she were seeking the invisible spirit that was communicating to me. I heard her uneven breath stopping and starting, following the rhythm of the drama; she sounded at times like someone climbing a mountain and pausing from time to time to catch her breath. By the time I reached the middle of the tale, the poor child had lost all her half-wild reserve with me. I could feel the warmth of her breathing on my hands. Her hair brushed my face. Two or three teardrops ran down her cheeks and fell, making tiny stains on the pages, right beside my fingers.

XIV

Except for my slow, dispassionate voice, literally translating that poem of the heart to the family of fishermen, the only other sounds were the low, far-off waves of the sea, beating against the rocks far below. And even that sound was in harmony with the reading. It was like the foreshadowing of the tale's denouement, moaning in advance in the air throughout the telling of the story. The further the story progressed, the more attached my listeners became. When I hesitated, now and then, trying to find the right expression to use for the French word, Graziella—who for some time now had been holding the lamp and shielding it from the wind with her apron—would get even closer to the pages, the lamp practically burning the book up with her impatience, as if she thought that bringing the light from the lamp closer would also bring me intellectual clarity and make the words spring more rapidly to my lips. I would smile and push the lamp away with my hand, without taking my gaze away from the page, and I could feel the hot tears on my fingers.

XV

When I got to the moment when Virginie, recalled to France by her aunt, begins to feel her very soul being rent in two and forces herself to console Paul under the banana trees, telling him she would return, pointing to the sea that would bring her back, I closed the book and said I would resume the reading the next day.

This fell like a blow upon the poor listeners. Graziella got onto her knees before me, and then before my friend, begging us to finish the story. But it was in vain. We wanted to prolong her interest, and our own pleasure in observing it. She tore the book out of my hands. She opened it, as if by sheer force of will she would be able to decipher the characters. She spoke to it, she kissed it. She then placed it respectfully back onto my knees, raising her joined hands to me like a supplicant.

Her face, normally so serene and smiling, though in an austere way, had now, from the story's passion and tenderness, taken on suddenly some of its wildness and pathos. It was as if some subtle alteration had turned a beautiful marble statue into flesh and tears. The girl felt her soul, which had lain asleep within her until now, begin to awaken, through the soul of Virginie. She seemed to have aged by six years or so in the course of the past half an hour. Her forehead now was tinted with the stormy hues of passion, as were the white purities of her eyes and cheeks. It was like a calm and sheltered pond when the sun, wind, and shadows come to battle with it for the first time. We could not stop looking at her. The girl who until now had only seemed a pleasant companion now inspired us with respect. But conjuring us to continue was in vain; we were determined to exercise our power over her more than just this once, and those beautiful tears of hers pleased us too much to let them all be used up in a single day. She got up at last with a pout and angrily blew out the lamp.

XVI

The next day, when I saw her among the vines and wanted to speak with her, she turned away as if she were hiding her tears and refused to reply to me. It was plain from the slight circles under her eyes, the increased pallor of her complexion, and the slight frown at the corners of her mouth that she had not slept and that her heart was still full of the imaginary sorrows from the night before. Oh, marvelous power of a book, that can work so on the heart of an unlettered child and her family with all the force of reality—and the reading of which is an event in the history of their hearts!

And in the same way that I had translated the poem, the poem had translated nature, and all those simple events—the cradles of the two children at the feet of their poor mothers, their innocent love, their cruel separation, their reunion foiled by death, the shipwreck, and the two graves beneath the banana trees holding but a single heart—all these are things that everyone knows and can understand, from those who live in palaces to those who live in a fisherman's cabin.[5] Poets seek everywhere for genius, whereas it resides within their hearts, and a few simple chords, played with reverence and without much planning, upon this instrument created by God Himself, will suffice to set a whole century weeping, and to become as popular as love and as sympathetic as feeling. The sublime can fail, the beautiful can deceive; pathos alone is infallible in art. The artist who knows how to touch our feelings knows everything. There is more genius in a tear than in all the museums and libraries of the universe. Man is like a tree that one shakes to make its fruits fall; whenever the man is touched, tears will follow.

XVII

All day long, the house was as sad as if some unfortunate event had befallen the humble family. People came together to eat their meals but barely spoke. Then they went their separate ways. When they encountered each other, they did not smile. We could tell that Graziella's heart was not in her tasks in the garden or up on the roof. She kept checking to see if the sun was beginning to go down, and it was obvious that she was waiting only for the evening to come.

And when it did come and we had all taken our normal places on the *astrico*, I reopened the book, and I completed telling the story, amid sobs. Father, mother, children, my friend, I myself—we all participated in the general emotion. The somber, serious tone of my voice blended, without my realizing it, with the sorrow of the events and the gravity of the words. By the end of the story those words seemed to be coming from afar, to be falling from above into our souls with a hollow sound, as if into an empty breast, where the heart no longer beats and which no longer participates in the things of the earth except through sorrow, religion, and memory.

XVIII

We found it impossible to make idle conversation after the story. Graziella remained motionless, in the posture she had adopted while listening, as if she were listening still. Silence—that applause given to enduring, true impressions—was interrupted by no one. Each respected the thoughts of the others, assuming they were like his or her own. The lamp burned down and went out without any of us picking it up to relight it. The family rose and went off to bed quietly. My friend and I remained alone, confounded by the almighty power of truth, simplicity, and sentiment upon all people, upon all ages, and in all lands.

And another emotion, perhaps, was beginning to stir in the depths of our hearts. The ravishing image of Graziella transfigured by tears, initiated into love by sorrow, floated in our consciousness along with the heavenly creation of Virginie. Those two names, those two girls, blending together in floating, drifting visions, enchanted and saddened our troubled sleep until the morning. On the evening of that next day and of the two that followed, we were persuaded to reread the same story twice over. We could have read it a hundred times, and she would still have asked for it again. The southern imagination is marked by deep reverie and is not interested in variety whether in poetry or in music; for such people, music and poetry are only themes through which each listener weaves his or her own sentiments; they nourish themselves, never sated, on the same story and the same tune for centuries.

But then, Nature herself, who is the supreme poetry and music—what does she have except for two or three words, two or three notes, always the same, with which she saddens or enchants us, from our first sigh to our final one?

XIX

At sunrise on the ninth day, the equinoctial winds at last began to fall, and the sea once again became a summer sea. Even the mountains on the Naples coast, like the waters and the sky, seemed to float suspended in a more limpid, bluer fluid than during the months of great heat—as if the sea, the sky, and the mountains already had felt the first shiver of winter, which crystallizes the air and makes it sparkle like the frozen waters of the glaciers. The yellowing leaves of the vines and the browning leaves of the fig trees began to fall and litter across the courtyard. The grapes had been picked. The figs, dried on the *astrico* in the sunlight, were packed in big baskets made of seaweed, woven and knotted together by the women. The boat was ready to try the sea, and the old fisherman prepared to bring his family to Margellina. They cleaned the house and the roof, covering the spring with a great stone so that the dry leaves and the rains of winter would not pollute the water. They took the oil out of the little well drilled into the rock and put it into jars; the children carried them down to the sea, using sticks passed between the handles. We put a great packet together of the mattresses and bedding, tying it with ropes. We lit the lamp, for one last time, under the abandoned image of the Madonna in the foyer. One last prayer was said before her, asking her to take under her protection the house, the fig trees, and the vines, which they would all be leaving for several months. Then they closed the door. They hid the key under the edge of an ivy-covered rock so that the fisherman, if he returned to his house during the winter, would know where to find it. Then we all descended to the water's edge, helping the poor family carry the oil, the breads, and the fruits, and to get them all stowed on board.

3

I

Our return to Naples, passing along the gulf of Baia and below the sinuous heights of Pausilippo, was a veritable celebration for the girl, the children, and for us, and it was a triumph for Andrea. We arrived at Margellina as night fell, singing as we went. The fisherman's old friends and relatives all came out to admire his new boat, and they helped him haul it up onto the beach. We had forbidden him to say who gave it to him, so no one paid much attention to us.

After getting the boat safely positioned on the beach, and after having carried the baskets of grapes and figs to Andrea's cellar, above which were the three low chambers in which his old wife, the children, and Graziella would sleep, we retired unobserved. We passed through the noisy, populous streets of Naples, not without feeling a certain clutching at our hearts, and we finally reentered our lodgings.

II

We decided, after several days of rest in Naples, to try to resume our life with the fisherman, whenever the sea would allow it. We had grown so accustomed to the simplicity of our clothing and the nakedness of the boat for the past three months that our beds, our furnishings, our rooms, and our town clothes now seemed annoying, fussy luxuries to us. We hoped we could leave them behind shortly. But the next day, when we went out to see if there had been any mail for us, my friend found a letter from his mother. She told her son to return to France immediately, to attend the wedding of his sister. His brother-in-law was to come as far as Rome to meet him. We considered the letter's date and thought that he must have arrived by now. There could be no delay: he would have to leave.

I should have gone with him. I'm not sure what desire for solitude or thirst for adventure kept me back. The life of a seaman, the fisherman's modest house, the image of Graziella—they all figured in somehow, but confusedly. And I could also name further reasons: the vertigo of freedom, pride in being capable of taking care of myself three hundred leagues from my home, a passion for the vague and the unknown, and the airy perspective that youthful imagination provides.

We parted with masculine warmth toward each other. He promised to come and rejoin me as soon as he had fulfilled his duties as a son and a brother. He lent me fifty louis to fill the hole these six months had made in my finances, and off he went.

III

That departure, the absence of my friend, who had been important to me in the way that an older brother is to a young boy, left me entirely isolated, and my loneliness increased as the hours passed; I felt as if I were at the edge of an abyss. All my thoughts and feelings, all my words, which had been freed to evaporate in constant exchanges with him, now remained within me and became corrupted, depressing me, resting on me like a weight I could not throw off. Nothing in all that noise interested me, no one in all that crowd knew my name, nothing in that room responded to my gaze, nothing in that inn felt right to me, where I was constantly being elbowed aside by strangers and where I ate my meals every day beside some new and indifferent people. And then the books that I had read a hundred times, whose unchanging characters say the same things and use the same expressions and always at the same place—all these had seemed so delicious in Rome and Naples, before our excursions, before our free, vagabond, wandering summer life, but now were like a slow death. My heart was steeped in melancholy.

I carried that sadness along with me from street to street, theater to theater, and finally it conquered me. I fell ill from that disease they call homesickness. My head was heavy, and my legs would barely support me. I was pale and haggard. I couldn't eat. Silence depressed me, and noise made me feel ill; I spent both days and sleepless nights on my bed, with neither the desire nor the strength to get up. The old relative of my mother, the only one there who could possibly have taken any interest in me, had gone to spend a few months thirty leagues from Naples in Abruzzo, where he planned to establish a factory. I asked for a doctor; he came, examined me, took my pulse, and told me there was nothing wrong with me. The truth was that I had a disease that medicine could not cure, a disease of the soul and the imagination. He left. I didn't see him again.

IV

But the next day I felt so bad that I began to ransack my memory to think of someone I could ask for help, or for pity at least, if I became unable to get up anymore. The image of the poor fisherman's family in Margellina arose naturally before me, and it was as if I still lived among them in memory. I sent a boy to look for Andrea and tell him that the younger of his two foreigners was ill and asking to see him.

When the boy delivered my message, Andrea and Beppino were out at sea; the grandmother was busy selling fish on the quays of Chiaia. Only Graziella was in the house, along with her little brothers. In hardly any time at all, she arranged for the children to stay with a neighbor, put on her best clothes, and, following the boy who showed her to my street, hurried up the stairs.

I heard a gentle knocking on my door. The door opened as if pushed inward by an invisible hand, and I saw Graziella. She cried out with alarm when she saw me and rushed forward several steps toward my bed; then, collecting herself and standing upright, she interlaced her fingers and let her hands hang before her on her apron, her head tilted to the left in the posture of Pity: "How pale he is!" she muttered. "And how short a time has passed to change him so!" Then out loud she asked, "And where is the other one?"

"He is gone," I said, "and I am alone, with no one in Naples."

"Gone?" she asked. "And he left you alone and sick like this? He must not love you! If I were in his place, I would never have left, even though I'm not your brother, and I've only known you since the day of the great storm!"

V

I explained that I had not been ill when my friend had departed. "But why," she went on in a tone that was half-reproach and half-tenderness, "didn't you call upon your friends in Margellina?" And then, glancing down at her dress and its sleeves, "Oh, I see," she said sadly. "It's because we're poor people and we would shame you if we came into this fine house. But still," she went on, wiping her eyes, and continuing to gaze upon me in my enfeebled state, "even if we'd have been rejected, we would have come to you anyway."

"Poor Graziella," I said to her with a smile. "God keep me from the day when I would feel ashamed of someone who loved me!"

VI

She sat down in a chair beside my bed, and we talked together for a while.

The sound of her voice, the serenity in her eyes, the trusting, calm freedom of her posture, the naïveté in her face, that halting but plaintive tone used by the women of the islands—a tone submissive, like that of a slave throbbing with love—and above all the memory of the fine days passed in the sunshine and the island house with her, that Procida sun that seemed still to be warming her forehead, her body, and her bare feet in my somber room: all this, while I listened and looked, lifted my spirits so entirely that I felt I had been suddenly cured. I felt I would be able to get up and walk as soon as she had left. But her presence made me feel so good that I prolonged the conversation and kept her there using a thousand pretexts, for fear that she might go too soon and take away my newfound health with her.

She took care of me for part of that day without fear, without any affected reserve, without any false modesty, like a sister caring for her brother, without any thought that he happened to be a man. She went out to buy me oranges. She bit off the rind with her beautiful teeth and used her fingers to squeeze some juice from them into my glass. She took off a little silver medallion that hung around her neck on a black silk thread, concealed between her breasts. She pinned it to the white curtain of my bed, assuring me that the holy image would very soon bring me back to health. Then, when the sun began to go down, she left, but not before repeatedly coming back from the door to my bed to ask me if there was anything I wanted and to insist that I pray devoutly to the image before going to sleep.

VII

Whether it was the image or the prayers that she herself no doubt prayed for me, whether it was the apparition of such tenderness and interest that I had felt from Graziella's visit, or whether it was the charming distraction that her presence and her conversation made to my weakened and sickly state, she had scarcely departed when I fell into a deep and peaceful sleep.

The next day, when I awoke, I saw the orange peels scattered on my floor, and the chair where Graziella had sat still turned toward my bed, as if she were still there; and I saw the little medallion hanging from my curtain by its black silk thread, and all the traces of a woman's presence and care, care I had been lacking for so long. All this at first confused me and made me think that my mother or one of my sisters must have come into my room overnight. It was only when my eyes fully opened that I was able to recall, one memory at a time, the way Graziella had come in, and the way she looked the day before.

The sun was so pure, and my sleep had so strengthened my limbs, and the solitude of my room weighed so heavily on my heart, and the need to hear the sound of her voice again was so strong that I soon got up, weak and trembling though I was; I ate the remainder of the oranges; I went down to the square and got into a *corricolo* and as if by instinct told the driver to take me to the coast of Margellina.

VIII

When I arrived at Andrea's low little house, I climbed up the stairs that led to the platform above his cellar, where the family's rooms were. And there on the *astrico* I found Graziella, the grandmother, the old fisherman, Beppino, and the children. As it happened, they were all getting ready to come see me, wearing their very best clothes. Each of them carried, in a basket, a kerchief, or simply in their hands, a present for me, something that the poor family thought would be best for a sick man: one had a flask of Ischia white wine stoppered with a plug of rosemary and aromatic herbs, instead of a cork, which perfumed the wine; another had some dried figs; another some medlar fruits; and the children, some oranges. The heart of Graziella had passed into all the members of her family.

IX

They all exclaimed in surprise to see me appearing there, still pale and weak, but on my feet and smiling. Out of joy, Graziella let the oranges she was carrying in her apron fall and roll onto the floor, and clapping her hands together, she ran up to me: "I told you!" she exclaimed. "I told you that image would cure you if she slept for one night on your bed. Wasn't I right?"

I took the medallion from my chest where I had worn it that morning. "Oh, kiss it first," she told me. I did kiss it, and the tips of those fingers of hers too, just a little, for she had extended them toward me to take the medallion. "I'll give it back to you if you fall sick again," she added, putting it around her neck and slipping it down between her breasts. "It will work for both of us."

We sat down on the terrace in the morning sun. The whole family had a kind of joy about them, as if they had recovered a long lost brother or a son who had been on a long voyage. Time is very important in forming intimate relationships among the upper classes, but not at all among the lower ones. Hearts there are open without mistrust, and they can bond together quickly, for there is no fear of hidden agendas in friendships and attachments. Close connections are forged in a week among such classes, connections that would take at least ten years to evolve with society people. I was already a member of this family.

We all told each other what we had been doing and what had happened to us, both good and bad, since we had been separated. The poor little house was in a state of perfect good fortune. The new boat had been blessed. The nets were full. Never had there been so many fish. The grandmother alone could not handle all the traffic selling fish to all the people who stopped at their door; Beppino was proud and strong and, though he was only twelve, he did the work of a twenty-year-old sailor. Graziella was in the process of learning a trade that would place her well above the humble status of her family. Her salary, already high for a young girl with the promise of rising even higher because of her talent, went toward clothing and feeding her little brothers, and it would also form a dowry for her, when she reached the age and inclination for love.

Those were the words of her grandparents. She was learning to be a *curallaro*, a coral worker. At that time, the industry involving the sale and manufacture of coral work formed the principal source of wealth for towns on the Italian coast. One of Graziella's uncles, brother to the mother she had lost, was a supervisor in the largest coral factory in Naples. Already rich for a man of his social class, and in charge of a number of workers both male and female, though there were never enough to supply the European demand for this luxury item, he had thought of his niece, and a few days earlier he had come around to recruit her as one of his workers. He had brought her some coral, and the necessary tools, and had given her basic lessons on how to execute this very simple art. His other female employees all did their work at the factory.

Because of the continual and necessary absence during the day of both the grandmother and the fisherman, Graziella was the sole caretaker for the children, and therefore she did her coral work at the house. Her uncle, who could not absent himself from the factory very often, had been sending his eldest son, Graziella's cousin, to oversee her work. He was a young man of twenty, intelligent enough, modest, capable, and a good worker, but somewhat simple-minded, scrawny, and slightly deformed in body. He would come in the evenings, after the factory had closed, to examine his cousin's work, help her improve in her use of the tools, and also to give her basic lessons in reading, writing, and arithmetic. "Let us hope," the grandmother whispered to me quietly while Graziella was not looking, "that this will work to the advantage of both, and that the supervisor will become the servant of his fiancée." I could see a grain of pride and ambition for her granddaughter in the old woman's thinking. But Graziella did not suspect anything.

X

She took me by the hand and led me to her room so that I could admire all the little coral pieces she had already turned and polished. They were all laid out on strips of cotton in little boxes at the foot of her bed. She wanted to make a coral piece for me. Sitting facing her, I turned the wheel of her little machine with my foot while she held the red coral branch up against the circular saw that ground and cut it. Then she rounded the pieces off by

Graziella / 73

holding them with the tips of her fingers up against the grindstone.

Pink dust covered her hands and, flying up from time to time toward her face, sprinkled her cheeks like a thin layer of cosmetic, making her eyes seem even bluer and more resplendent. Then she laughed and wiped off her face, shaking the dust out of her black hair, which in turn covered me in it.

"Isn't this the perfect thing for a girl of the sea, like me? You know, we owe everything to the sea: from my grandfather's boat to the bread we eat to these necklaces and earrings that I might wear myself someday, when I've shaped and polished enough of them for women who are richer and prettier than I am."

And so the morning passed, in a mix of work and playful conversation, and the idea of leaving never occurred to me. At noon I shared in the family's meal. The sun, the fresh air, the sense of contentment, the frugality of the table, with only some bread, fried fish, and preserved fruits from the cellar—all this combined to give me an appetite and to bring my strength back. In the afternoon I helped the old man mend a net that he had spread out on the *astrico*. Our work was accompanied by the low, melodious sounds of Graziella turning her grindstone, of the grandmother's spinning wheel, and the voices of the little ones playing with oranges out on the doorstep. From time to time Graziella would come and shake out her hair on the balcony, and we would exchange a glance, a friendly word, a smile. I felt happy, without knowing why, happy to the depths of my soul. I could have wanted to be one of the aloe plants rooted around the garden fence, or one of the lizards that was sunning itself next to us on the terrace and that lived with the poor family in the crevices of their walls.

XI

But as day turned to evening, my mind and my expression both became more somber. I felt saddened, thinking of having to return to my traveler's room. Graziella was the first one to notice it. She went and spoke a few quiet words in the ear of her grandmother.

"Why should we separate like this?" asked the old woman, as if she were talking about one of her children. "Didn't we all live together on Procida? And aren't we the same, here in Naples? You look like a bird who's lost his mother and is flying around all the other nests crying. Come and live in ours—that is, if you think it's good enough for a fine *monsieur* like yourself. We only have three rooms, but Beppino can sleep in the boat. Graziella can double up with the children, as long as she can come in and work in the room where you sleep. You take her room and stay here until your friend returns. Because a good young man like you, sad and all alone in the streets of Naples—it's painful to think of it."

The fisherman, Beppino, and even the little ones, who already loved the foreigner, all rejoiced at her idea. They insisted vigorously altogether that I accept the offer. Graziella said nothing, but she awaited with visible anxiety, though she tried to hide it, my response to her family's invitation. She stomped her foot in an involuntary way at every one of the discreet and polite reasons I gave for not accepting.

Finally, I looked up and directly at her. I saw that her eyes were moister and more brilliant than they usually were, and that she was unconsciously fingering and crushing the leaves of a basil plant that grew in an earthenware pot there on the balcony. That gesture said more to me than a long speech could have. I accepted the community and the life they were offering me. Graziella clapped her hands and skipped for joy as she ran back into her room; she did not return, as if she wanted to be sure that I kept my word and was not going to give me the chance to change my mind.

XII

Graziella called Beppino. In almost no time, she and her brother carried into the children's room her bed, her few furnishings, her little mirror in its painted wooden frame, her brass lamp, the two or three images of the Virgin that she had attached with pins to her walls, her table, and the little wheel with which she worked her coral. They drew water from the well and spread it around the floor using the palms of their hands, sweeping away carefully the coral powder from the wall and the stone floor. They balanced in the windowsill the two greenest and most fragrant pots of mint and reseda that they could find out on the *astrico*. They would not have made more preparations or taken more care if this were a bridal chamber and Beppo were bringing his bride to the house of his father. I helped them, the three of us laughing as we worked.

When everything was ready, I brought Beppino and the fisherman with me to buy and carry home a few necessary furnishings. I bought a little iron bed, a table of white wood, two rush-bottomed chairs, and a little brass pan for heating olive stones during winter evenings, which was the custom for heating one's room. My suitcase, fetched from my rented room, contained everything else. I was not willing to lose a single night of this happy life with what seemed my new family. I only awoke the next morning when I heard the joyful cries of the swallows, which entered my room through a window with a broken pane, and the voice of Graziella, who was singing in the room next door, accompanying her song with the rhythmic movement of her wheel.

XIII

I opened the window, looking out on the little gardens of fishermen and washerwomen tucked into the rocks of Mount Pausilippo and the square of Margellina.

Some blocks of brown sandstone had rolled down into those gardens, quite close to the house. Big fig trees, their roots half-crushed under these rocks, were growing so as to seize hold of them with their great, white, twisted arms, covering them with large, motionless leaves. From this side of the house, I could see the gardens of those poor people, and wells with great wheels attached, being slowly turned by a donkey in order to irrigate gutters running between rows of fennel, thin cabbages, and turnips; and women, drying their washing on ropes strung from one lemon tree to another; little children, too, in shirts playing or crying up on the terraces of two or three small white houses, scattered among all the gardens. This view, so limited, so ordinary, and so simple, the outskirts of a large city, seemed delicious to me in comparison to the hemmed-in streets and the raucous crowd noise of the neighborhood where I had been living. I breathed in the pure air, instead of the dust, heat, and smoke of the human atmosphere I had been inhaling. I could hear donkeys braying, roosters crowing, the rustle of leaves, and the groanings of the sea, instead of the creaking of wheels on pavement and the shrill cries of people and the incessant thunder of all those strident city noises that never allow a person a little quiet or space to think.

I could not drag myself out of my bed to end the delicious savor of that sun, those country sounds, the rustle of the birds, the unruffled peace of mind; and then, looking around at the bareness of the walls, the emptiness of the room, the absence of furniture, I rejoiced in the thought that the people of this poor house loved me, and no fine carpets or silk curtains were worth anything like that simple attachment. All the gold in the world would not buy a single beam of tenderness in the gaze of indifferent people.

I lay cradled in such thoughts, half-asleep; I could feel health and peace renewing within me. Beppino came into my room several times to see if I needed anything. He brought me some bread and some grapes, which I ate while tossing crumbs to the swallows. It was almost noon. The sun was shining brightly in my room with the gentle warmth of autumn when I finally got up. I spoke with the fisherman and his wife, settling on a figure for rent that I would give them each month for my room and board, as a contribution to household expenses. It was small enough, but for those fine people it seemed too much. Anyone could see that, far from trying to profit from me, they suffered inwardly because their poverty and frugal life would not permit them to offer me the kind of hospitality that they would have been more proud of if they could have offered it to me at no cost. They added two loaves of bread to what they usually bought each morning for the family, a little boiled or fried fish for dinner, some milk and dried fruits for the evening, oil for my lamp, and coals for cold days: that was all. A few copper *grano* coins, used in Naples, were enough for my daily expenses. I had never before learned how little happiness has to do with luxury, and how much more one can buy with a little bit of copper than with a purse full of gold, when one knows where to find what God has hidden.

XIV

I lived thus for the last months of autumn and the first months of winter. The radiance and serenity of those months in Naples make me confuse them with the preceding ones. Nothing troubled the even tranquility of our lives. The old man and his grandson no longer went out to the open sea because of the high winds that the season brought with it. But they did continue fishing closer along the coast, and the grandmother selling their catch along the *marine* met all their needs.

Graziella grew more perfect in her art; and she grew and developed more perfectly still in her life, the sweeter, more sedentary life she had been leading since she began working with coral. Her wages, brought to her on Sundays by her uncle, allowed her not only to dress her little brothers better and to send them to school, but also to give to her grandmother—and to herself—some of the finer, more elegant clothing items worn by women of their island: kerchiefs of red silk that hang down over the head and in a long triangular shape down the shoulders; little shoes without heels that cover only the toes, embroidered with silver sequins; black-and-green-striped silk vests, trimmed at the seams and floating open at the hips, allowing one to see the shape of the waist and the contours of the neck, adorned with necklaces; and finally, large carved earrings with golden threads setting off pearls. The poorest women of the Greek isles wear these sorts of ornaments. No financial distress would ever induce them to part with them. In climates where the feeling for beauty is stronger than it is under our northern skies, and where life is nothing more than love, such ornaments are not luxuries in a woman's view: they are her first and almost her only necessity.

XV

When, on Sundays or holidays, Graziella thus dressed would come out of her room onto the terrace, with some orange pomegranate flowers or laurel roses tucked into her black hair on one side; when, hearing the sound of the bells in the nearby chapel, she would pass and repass in front of my room like a peacock basking in the sun on the roof; when she would languidly drag her feet along, imprisoned in those spangled slippers, gazing down on them, and then would suddenly raise her head up with a graceful undulation of her neck that was typical of her and in doing so would cause the red silk kerchief to flutter in her hair and on her shoulders; when she could see that I was watching her, she would redden a little, as if she were ashamed at being so beautiful. There were moments when the radiance of her beauty stunned me, as if I were seeing her for the first time, and my normal familiarity with her would change into a bashful awkwardness.

But she tried so little to dazzle, and her natural instinct to ornament herself was so utterly exempt from pride or coquetry, that as soon as she returned from the religious ceremonies she would hasten to remove all her rich clothing and dress again in her simple vest of coarse green cloth, her cotton dress with red and black stripes, and her shoes with the white wooden heels, which sounded all day long on the terrace like those echoing slippers female slaves wear in the Orient.

When her young friends did not come by to fetch her, or her cousin failed to accompany her to church, it would often be up to me to escort her and wait for her, sitting outside on the church steps. When she would emerge, I would feel a kind of personal pride, as if she had been my sister or my fiancée, at hearing the murmurs of admiration that her graceful figure elicited from her companions or from the young sailors on the quays of Margellina. But she never heard any of it, and having eyes only for me among the crowd, would smile at me from the top step, making her last sign of the cross with her fingers still moist with holy water; she would come down the steps modestly, her eyes lowered, descending by degrees to where I awaited her.

And so it was that on holidays I would take her, morning and evening, to church, the sole and pious diversion she knew, and one she loved. I took care on those days to dress as much like the young sailors on the isle as I could so that my presence would surprise no one and so that they would all take me for a brother or for a relative of the girl I was accompanying.

On other days, she would not go out at all. As for me, I slowly reverted to my life of study and my solitary ways, distracted only by Graziella's sweet friendship and by the family's adoption of me. I read the historians and poets from all languages. Often, I was writing: I tried, sometimes in Italian, sometimes in French, to pour out in prose or verse those first effusions of the soul, those feelings that seem to weigh the heart down until given some release through words.

It seems that words are man's true destination and that we were created to give birth to thoughts the way a tree gives birth to its fruit. A man is in torment until he has produced outside of himself that which was laboring within him. Our written words are like mirrors, mirrors we need in order to know ourselves and to assure ourselves that we exist. If we have not seen ourselves in our works, we are not completely alive. The mind has its puberty, just as the body does.

I was at the age when the soul needs to nourish and multiply itself through language. But, as often happens, the instinct came to life within me before the power had. As soon as I had written something, I was discontented with it and I threw it away in disgust. How many of the rags and shreds of my nighttime feelings and thoughts have been consumed by the winds and the sea of Naples, when I had ripped them up in the morning and thrown them away, without regret, far away from me!

XVI

Sometimes Graziella, when she had seen me shutting myself in and being quieter than usual, would slip furtively into my room to try to coax me away from my stubborn reading or writing. She would come up quietly behind my chair, get up on her tiptoes in order to see over my shoulders what I was reading or writing, without being able to comprehend it; then, in a sudden movement, she would snatch my book away or steal the pen out of my fingers and then run off. I would pursue her onto the terrace, a little annoyed, and she would laugh at me. I would pardon her; but she would then rebuke me in all seriousness, as if she had been my mother.

"What has that book of yours been saying to you, that you've kept your eyes glued to it all day?" she would murmur, her impatience half-playful and half-serious. "Are those black lines on that white paper ever going to finish talking to you? Don't you already know enough stories to tell us a different one every Sunday for a year, like the one that made me cry so much back on Procida? And who are you writing those long letters to every night, the ones you rip up and throw out to the ocean winds? Can't you see that you're making yourself ill and that you go all pale and distracted when you've been writing or reading for such a long time? Isn't it nicer to come and talk with me, a real person who can look at you, instead of talking day and night with those words or those ghosts who never hear you? My God! Don't I have as much to offer as a sheet of paper? I would speak to you all day long, I would tell you anything you asked me, and you would never have to wear out your eyes or burn so much oil in your lamp." At that, she would go and hide my book and my pens. She would come back with my sailing jacket and cap and would force me to go outdoors to distract myself.

I grumbled as I obeyed her, but I also loved her as I did so.

I

I liked to take long walks across the town, onto the quays, out into the countryside; but these solitary rambles were not sad ones like those of the first days after my return to Naples. I enjoyed alone, but I did enjoy, and deliciously, the spectacles of the city, the shores, the sky, and the sea. The occasional feeling of aloneness no longer overwhelmed me; instead, it brought me back to myself and helped focus my feelings and my thoughts. I knew that the eyes and thoughts of friends followed me now, whether I walked through crowds or deserted country, and that when I returned, I would be waited for by hearts that cared for me.

So I was no longer like the bird crying out around the nests of strangers, to use the old woman's expression; instead, I was like the bird that tries to fly as far away as he can, pushing off from his branch, but always knowing the route to take to get back. All my affection for my absent friend now flowed over onto Graziella. If anything, the feeling was even stronger, sharper, deeper than the one I had been so close to. I thought that the difference was that the first friendship had been a connection born out of habit and circumstances while the other was born out of myself, that it was a connection I had chosen.

This was not love, for I experienced no agitation, no jealousy, nor any passionate preoccupation; it was, rather, a delicious repose for the heart, and not one of those sweet fevers of the soul and the senses. I never thought of loving in any other way, and I did not think about being loved. I didn't know if she was a comrade, a friend, a sister, or some other thing for me; I only knew that I was happy with her and that she was happy with me.

And I desired nothing more, nothing at all. I had not yet reached that age where one self-analyzes every feeling one feels in order to give some vain definition to one's sense of happiness. For me, it was enough to be calm, attached, and happy, without knowing what I was happy about or why. Life together, thinking alike, reaffirmed every day the innocence of the sweet familiarity between us, for she was as pure in her abandon as I was calm in my detachment.

II

During the three months I stayed with the family under the same roof, it was as if I had somehow become a part of her thought; Graziella had become so used to seeing me as inseparable from her heart that she perhaps did not know herself how large a part I had come to play there. With me, she never had any of those fears, those reserves, those moments of modesty that come between a young girl and a boy, and that often lead to the birth of love out of the very precautions taken against it. She never feared, nor did I, that the way her pure, childlike graces were blossoming more fully now with every day of sunshine and approaching a precocious maturity meant that her naive beauty could be used in some way by her, or be admired by others, or be a danger for me. She never tried either to hide it from me or display it to me. She thought no more than a sister would about whether her brother found her beautiful or ugly. She never put one flower more or less in her hair for me. She did not cover her bare feet with shoes any more frequently when, in the mornings, she would dress her little brothers out in the sunshine on the terrace, or when she would help her grandmother sweep away the dead leaves that had fallen overnight. She would enter my room at any hour, for it was always open, and would sit as innocently as Beppino on the chair at the foot of my bed.

On rainy days I would spend whole hours alone with her in the adjoining room where she slept with the little ones and where she worked with her coral. I would help her, chatting and joking, and she taught me the technique. Less adroit but stronger than she was, I could trim the pieces of coral faster. We doubled up the work, and she earned twice the wages for that day.

But in the evening, on the other hand, when the children and the family were in bed, it was she who became the pupil and I the teacher. I taught her to read and write by making her spell out the words in my books, and I took her hand in mine, guiding it to help her trace them. Her cousin could not come every day, so I substituted for him. Whether it was because that young man, misshapen and limping, did not inspire sufficient respect in her, despite her sweet nature, her patience, and the gravity of her manner; or because she had too many distractions during his lessons—in any case, she made far less progress with him than she did with me. With him, half the evening's study time would be taken up with laughter and with mocking her teacher. The poor young man was too smitten with her, and too timid, to complain. He did everything she wanted so that not a single wrinkle of bad humor would appear on the lovely forehead of his pupil and so that her superb lips would not shape themselves into a pout. Often, the hour that was supposed to be dedicated to reading ended up being used for whittling down the coral, or helping the grandmother sort the skeins of wool on her distaff, or aiding Beppo in repairing nets. Everything was good, in his eyes, so long as Graziella smiled at him when he left, saying *addio* to him in that tone that meant *au revoir.*

III

But when she was with me, on the contrary, the lesson was serious. Sometimes it would extend to the point where our eyes became heavy with sleep. Her drooping head, her bent neck, her intense, attentive, motionless posture and attitude all revealed how hard the poor child was trying to achieve success. She would lean her elbow on my shoulder in order to read from the book, on which my finger would be tracing the line and indicating the word she was to pronounce. When she practiced writing, I would take her fingers in my hand to guide her pen a little.

If she made a mistake, I grumbled in a severe, angry tone; she would not reply but instead become impatient with herself. Many times I saw her close to tears; at those moments I would soften my tone and encourage her to try again. And when she had read or written well, anyone could see that the only reward she wanted was my approbation. She would turn to me blushing, with joy radiating across her face and in her eyes, more proud of the pleasure she had given me than of the little victory she had made.

I would reward her by reading a few pages from *Paul et Virginie*, which she preferred above all else, or some fine stanzas from Tasso, in which he described the serene pastoral life that Herminia lived, or in which he sang of the pleadings or sorrows of lovers.[1] The music of those verses would make her weep and put her into a reverie that lasted long after I had ceased reading. Poetry has no more sonorous, more prolonged echo than in the heart of the young, where love is about to be born. It is like the foreshadowing of all the passions. And later in life, it is like the memory of them, and their funeral song. It brings tears, thus, to the two extreme eras in our lives: youth and hope, age and regret.

IV

The charm and the easy familiarity of those long, sweet evenings in the lamplight, the olive brazier warming our feet, never led us into any thoughts or intimacies different from the thoughts and intimacies of two children. Such thoughts were forbidden to us—to me, by my almost cold indifference, and to her by her openness and her natural modesty. We left each other as tranquilly as we had come together, and within a few moments of separating, we each were sound asleep, beneath the same roof and only a few feet from each other, exactly like two children who had been playing together in the evening and now were dreaming of nothing beyond their simple amusements. The calm state of enjoying feelings without analyzing them, feelings that nurture themselves, requiring no feeding from us—this state might have gone on like that for years, if it hadn't been for an event that changed everything and that revealed to us the true nature of a friendship that was all we needed for happiness.

V

Cecco—this was the name of Graziella's cousin—continued to come to the house, even more assiduously now, to spend the winter evenings with the family of the old *marinaro*. Even though she showed no preference toward him, and even though he was the butt of some jokes and even some satire from his cousin, he was so gentle, so patient, and so humble when he was around her that she could not fail to be touched by his kindnesses, and even to smile on him approvingly from time to time. And that was enough for him. He belonged to that type of person who has a weak but loving heart, the type of person who feels cut off by his very nature from the qualities that can make a person beloved and therefore contents himself with loving, with no expectation of being loved in return, and who devotes himself like a voluntary slave to the service, if not the happiness, of the woman who holds his heart in subjection. These are not the noblest types of human attachment, but they are the most touching. One grieves for them, but one also admires them. Loving in order to be loved: such is the natural state of man. But loving for the sake of loving: that is closer to the angels.

VI

And beneath his utterly graceless exterior, there actually was something angelic about the love of this poor Cecco. Far from feeling humiliated or jealous over the familiarities that passed between us and the clear preference that Graziella showed for me, instead he loved me because she loved me. He didn't ask to hold the first or the only place in his cousin's affections; second place, or even last place, would do: anything would suffice. If it would have given her a moment's pleasure, if it would have resulted in a kindly glance or gesture from her, he would have sought me out in the farthest corner of France and brought me— the one she preferred—to her. I believe he would have hated me if I had caused any pain to his cousin.

His pride was not in himself but in her, and so was his love. And it may have been true also that deep inside his cool, reflective, methodical mind he was willing to bet that my power over his cousin's affections would not be eternal; that some circumstance, some event of whatever kind would inevitably separate us; that I was a foreigner, from a distant country, born and raised within a social level entirely incompatible with that of a fisherman's daughter in Procida; that one day or another, the intimacy between his cousin and me would evaporate just as swiftly as it had formed; that then she would be left to him, all abandoned and forsaken; that her very despair would cause her heart to yield, and she would then turn to him and give him that heart of hers, broken but whole. That was the only role he could hope for, being the friend and the consoler. But his father had other ideas for him.

VII

The father, recognizing Cecco's attachment for his niece, would come to see her from time to time. Touched by her beauty and her intelligence, marveling at the rapid progress she was making in her coral work as well as in her reading and writing, and thinking that Cecco's inelegant appearance would never allow him to hope for any kind of love except the kind provided by family, he had resolved to marry his son and his niece. Having made his fortune, and quite a considerable one for a laborer, he felt entitled to regard this idea as something of a favor, and one that Andrea, his wife, and the girl herself could not possibly resist. Whether he had told Cecco about his project, or whether he had kept it secret as a surprise that would delight the son, he resolved now to speak about it with the family.

VIII

On Christmas Eve, I came home later than usual and took my place at the table for supper with the family. I sensed a kind of restraint in the air, and I could see from their faces that something was troubling Andrea and his wife. Turning to look at Graziella, I could see that she had been crying. Serenity and gaiety had been so habitual with her that now this unusual expression of sorrow seemed to cover her face like a veil. It was as if the shadow in her thoughts and her heart had spread out over her features. I waited, petrified and silent, not daring to ask questions of the old people or Graziella, for fear that the sound of my voice would shatter the restraint she was trying so hard to maintain.

Unusually for her, she did not look at me. She distractedly picked up a few bits of bread, trying to give the semblance of eating, but she was unable. She threw the pieces of bread under the table. When the silent meal came to an end, she got up under the pretext of getting the children ready for bed; she took them into their room; and she shut herself in there, without saying a word either to her family or to me, leaving us sitting there alone.

When she had gone, I asked the grandfather and grandmother what was making them so serious and their child so sad. They told me then that Cecco's father had come to the house that day and that he had asked for the hand of their granddaughter in marriage to his son; that this was a great good fortune for the family; that Cecco would inherit a great deal; that Graziella, who was so good, would take the two young children with her, just as if they were her own children; that in their own old age they would no longer have to fear poverty; that they had consented gratefully to this offer of marriage; that they had told Graziella about it; that she had said nothing in reply, out of a young woman's natural timidity and modesty; that her silence and her tears were only the effects of her surprise, and of the emotion it caused, but that all this would pass away like an insect flitting over a flower; and finally, that they, the father, and Cecco had all agreed that the engagement would be celebrated after the Christmas holidays.

IX

They continued talking for a long time, but I was no longer listening. I had never really tried to take the measure of my feelings for Graziella. I didn't know how much I loved her, or whether it was innocent intimacy, or friendship, or love, or simply habit, or maybe all those things combined, that comprised the way I felt about her. But now, the idea of seeing all these sweet, tender relations that had been established firmly and permanently in my life, and within my heart, without either of us quite being aware of it all; the thought that they were going to take her away from me and give her to someone else; the thought that the girl who was my companion, my sister, was to become a stranger to me, indifferent, that she would no longer be there, that soon I would no longer see her at any hour of the day, never again hear her voice calling to me, that I would no longer read that light in her eyes, that light always focused on me, that caressing, affectionate light that shone right down into my heart, and that recalled my mother and my sisters to my mind; the empty, endless night that I imagined would soon enfold me on the day after her husband came and took her away to his house; that room, where she would no longer lie sleeping; that table I would never again see her setting; the terrace where I would never again hear the gentle sound of her bare feet, or her morning voice calling to awaken me; those churches, where I would never again escort her on Sundays; the boat, where her spot would remain empty, and where I would never again converse with the wind and the waves—the images of all these sweet habits of our life together passed before me, flooding my thoughts and leaving me in what felt like an abyss of solitude and nothingness. All this made me feel, for the first time, just how much the presence of this girl had meant to me and clarified that, whether it was love or friendship, the feeling I had for her was far stronger than I had believed and that, unbeknownst to me, the charm of my wild life here outside Naples lay in neither the sea, nor the boat, nor the humble room in the house, nor the fisherman, his wife, or Beppo or the little ones: it was all concentrated in one single being, and if that being were to disappear, all the rest would disappear at once as well. She was my life, at the present; there was nothing else. I felt it: a feeling that had been only confused and vague till now, one that I had never confessed to myself, now struck me with such force that my heart shuddered, and I felt something of the infinity of love by virtue of the infinity of sorrow into which my heart now felt itself plunged.

X

I went back into my room without saying a word. I threw myself fully dressed upon my bed. I tried to read, to write, to think, to distract myself through some kind of painful, demanding effort that would help me get control over my agitation. Everything I tried was useless. My inner turmoil was so intense that I could not join two thoughts together, and the very exhaustion of my body would not let me sleep. The image of Graziella had never been so present to my mind's eye, and it had never been so ravishing. I had taken pleasure in it like something one sees every day, the sweetness of which only becomes clear after it is gone. Her beauty itself had not particularly touched me before this day; I had confused the impression it made on me with the effects of the friendship I felt for her, and with the friendship for me that her smile expressed. I had not realized how intense an attachment I felt for her; I never suspected that there was the slightest passion mixed within her tenderness.

Even now I could not fully account for it all, even during the long wanderings of my thoughts and heart all that sleepless night. Everything was confused, my sorrows and my thoughts. I was like a man stunned by a sudden blow, uncertain who struck him and why he is in pain, but who feels the pain nonetheless.

I arose from my bed before any sounds were heard in the house. I don't know what instinct it was that urged me to get away for a while, as if my presence, the presence of a stranger, would disturb the family sanctuary at such a moment.

I slipped out, telling Beppo that I would be gone for several days. I took the first pathway that presented itself to me. I passed along the quays of Naples, the Resina coast, then Portici, and then the base of Vesuvius. I hired some guides in Torre del Greco; I slept outside on a rock, at the door of the San Salvatore hermitage, at the borderline where the regions of inhabited nature end and the regions of fire begin. The volcano had been active for some time, and its every shudder shot up clouds of smoke as well as rocks, which we could hear all night long rolling into the ravine of lava near the hermitage; my guides therefore refused to go up any farther. I climbed up alone; with great effort, I ascended the uppermost cone, my hands and feet sunken in the thick ash that gave way under my weight. The volcano groaned and thundered. Burning rocks, still red, hailed down here and there around me, extinguishing themselves in the ashes. But nothing would stop me. I made my way to the very edge of the crater. I sat down. I watched the sun rise over the gulf, over the countryside, and over the glittering rooftops of Naples. I felt unmoved, coldly observing the spectacle that travelers come to see from such great distances. Within that great immensity of light, of seas, of coastlines, and of buildings struck by the rays of the sun, my eyes sought out a single white point visible among the green of surrounding trees, at the very extremity of Pausilippo, where I thought I could make out Andrea's little house. We try to observe and grasp space in vain; all of nature, for us, is composed of two or three points toward which our souls always tend. Remove the heart that loves you, and what remains of your life? It is the same with the world of nature. Take away the site and the house your thoughts are seeking, or the one populated by your memories, and all that remains is a great emptiness, and your gaze finds no bottom to it, no place of repose. Is it any surprise, then, that the most sublime scenes on earth should be viewed with so different an eye by different travelers? The reason is that in our travels we all carry with us our own point of view. A cloud over the heart covers and darkens the earth more than a cloud in the sky does. The spectacle is in the spectator. I have felt this.

XI

I looked upon it all; I saw nothing. In vain I climbed down, like a madman, clutching at outcroppings of cooled lava, until I reached the floor of the crater. In vain I managed to cross over deep crevasses, billowing forth smoke and flame that blinded and scorched me. In vain I contemplated those great fields of sulfur and crystallized salt that look like glaciers but are colored by the hot breath of the fires. I was indifferent to wonder, indifferent to danger. My heart was elsewhere; I tried in vain to bring it back.

In the evening, I made my way back down to the hermitage. I dismissed my guides; I crossed the vineyards toward Pompeii. I spent a whole day wandering the ruins of that buried city. That great tomb, open now for two thousand years and revealing its streets, its monuments, its arts to the sun and sky—all this left me as unmoved as Vesuvius had. The soul of all those ashes had been swept away so thoroughly over the centuries by the winds of God that it no longer spoke to my heart. I walked through the dust of human beings in the streets of what had once been their city with as much indifference as if it had been a heap of empty shells cast upon the seashore. Time is a great ocean that, just like the other ocean, overflows and casts up our debris. No one can weep over everything. Each of us has his sorrows, and each century has its pity; it is best this way.

When I left Pompeii, I pushed forward into the woody mountain gorges of Castellammare and Sorrento. I stayed there several days, wandering from one village to another, asking the goat herders to point me toward the most celebrated spots. They took me for a painter seeking out viewpoints, for I would take notes from time to time in a little book of drawings that my friend had given me. But I was nothing more than a wandering soul, rambling the countryside from here to there to kill some days. Nothing was any good to me. I was no good to myself.

I could not go on like this for much longer. When the Christmas season had passed and the first of the year came, that day that people make into a holiday as if to seduce and sway Time with toys and wreaths, as if trying to soften a severe host with charm, I hurried to get back to Naples. I got there at nightfall, and I hesitated, torn between my impatience to see Graziella and the terror of learning that I would never see her again. I stopped twenty times; I sat down on the side of a boat as I approached Margellina.

I ran into Beppo a little way from the house. He shouted for joy at seeing me, and he rushed to embrace me like a little brother. He brought me to his boat while telling me what had happened in my absence.

Everything had changed in the house. Graziella did nothing but weep ever since I left. She never came to the table for meals. She stopped working with her coral. She spent all day closed up in her room, rarely replying to anyone who called her, and she spent her nights pacing on the terrace. People in the neighborhood were saying that she was either crazy or had fallen *innamorata*. But he knew very well that wasn't true.

All this trouble arose, the boy continued, from their trying to get her married to Cecco, which she didn't want to do. Beppino had seen and heard everything. Cecco's father came every day asking for an answer from the grandfather and grandmother. They never stopped tormenting Graziella, trying to get her to consent. She didn't want to even hear them talk about it; she said she would rather run off to Geneva. For the Catholic people of Naples, that's an expression meaning, roughly, I would rather be an apostate. It's a stronger threat even than that of suicide, because it implies the eternal suicide of the soul. Andrea and his wife, who both adored Graziella, despaired both at her resistance and at the dashing of the hopes they had had for her future security. They implored her, invoking their white hair; they spoke to her about their old age, their poverty, the future of the two little ones. Finally, Graziella softened. She treated poor Cecco a little more kindly when he came, from time to time, to sit down humbly in the evening outside his cousin's door and play with the little ones. He would say hello and goodbye through the door, but only rarely did she speak a single word in reply. He would go off, discontented but resigned, and would come back the next day always the same. "My sister is very wrong," Beppino said. "Cecco loves her so much, and he is so good! She would be so happy!

"Tonight at last," he continued, "she let herself be

won over by the prayers of my grandfather and grandmother, and by the tears of Cecco. She opened the door just a little; she extended her hand to him; he slipped a ring on her finger, and she promised that she would be engaged to him tomorrow. But who knows if she'll have some new whim tomorrow? She used to be so sweet, and so happy! My God, how she's changed. You would hardly recognize her!"

XII

Beppino curled up to sleep in the boat. Thus instructed by him as to what had been happening, I went up into the house.

Andrea and his wife were alone on the *astrico*. They caught sight of me and with great friendliness began to heap gentle reproaches on me for my too-prolonged absence. They told me all about their troubles and hopes with regard to Graziella. "If you had been here," Andrea said, "since you're the one she likes so much, the one she never says no to, you could have been a real help to us. Oh, we're so glad to see you again! Tomorrow is the official betrothal; you'll be there; your presence has always been good luck for us."

I felt a shudder go through my whole body at these words from those poor old people. Something inside told me that all their troubles had their roots in me. I was burning to see Graziella again, and I trembled with fear to see her. I made a point of speaking quite loudly to her grandparents and of walking back and forth in front of her door; I didn't want to call to her, but I wanted to be heard. She remained utterly silent and did not appear. I went into my room and lay down. A certain calm descended upon me, the kind we feel when certitude—even certitude of misery—replaces a restless, agitated state of doubt. I lay on the bed like a dead weight, motionless. The fatigue of my mind and body plunged me immediately into confused dreams, and then into the nothingness of sleep.

XIII

Two or three times during the night I partly woke up. It was one of those winter nights rare in warm, seaside climates, but all the more sinister for such a setting. Lightning flashed constantly through the closed shutters of my window, like the blinking of a fiery eye on the wall of my room. The wind groaned like the howls of starving dogs. Low heavy thuds of the waves breaking upon the beach of Margellina echoed and resounded, as if someone were hurling massive rocks.

My door shuddered and rattled in the wind. Two or three times I thought it was opening, and then it closed by itself, and I thought I could hear human sobbing amid the wailing of the storm. Once I even thought I heard words, and my name being called by someone crying out for help; I rose up at once; I heard nothing more; I concluded that the storm, my fever, and my dreams were all pulling me into their illusions; I fell back into a heavy sleep.

In the morning, the tempest gave place to the purest sunshine. But now I was awakened by real groans and by cries of despair from the poor fisherman and his wife who were crying out as they stood on the threshold outside Graziella's room. The poor girl had fled during the night. She had got up, embraced the children, and signed to them to say nothing. She had left behind on her bed all her finest clothes, her earrings, her necklaces, and the little money she had.

The grandfather was holding a piece of paper dripping with rainwater that they had found pinned to her bed. There were five or six lines that they begged me desperately to read. I took the sheet of paper. On it were only these words, written feverishly, so that I could barely make them out: "I have promised too much . . . a voice has told me that it's stronger than I am. I kiss your feet; I beg your forgiveness. I will become a nun. Please console Cecco and the *Monsieur* . . . I will pray to God for him and for the little ones. Give them everything I have. Return the ring to Cecco. . . ."

As I read these lines, the whole family again burst into tears. The little children, still undressed, understood that their sister had left them forever, and their wailing mixed with the sobs of the old people, the sound traversing all through the house and calling out, Graziella!

XIV

The note fell from my hands. As I bent to pick it up, I saw on the ground, under my door, a pomegranate flower—the one I had admired, on a Sunday, in her hair—and lying there, too, was the little medallion she always wore on her breast, the one she had pinned to my curtain months ago, when I had been ill. Now I knew that my door had indeed been opened and shut during the night, and that the stifled sobs and moans I thought I had heard, and that I took for effects of the wind, were in fact the sobs and farewells of the poor girl. A dry patch on the door's lintel at the entry to my bedroom, a sole dry spot where so much rain had fallen, attested to her having sat there during the storm; she must have spent her last hours here weeping, sitting or kneeling on this spot. I picked up the pomegranate flower and the medallion and hid them away.

The poor family, amid their despair, were touched to see me weeping just like them. I did what I could to console them. All agreed that if they were able to find the girl, there would be no more talk of Cecco. Cecco himself, whom Beppo had sought out, was the first to sacrifice himself to the peace of the house and the return of his cousin. Distraught as he was, one could see that he was happy to hear that his name had been mentioned with some tenderness in the note and that he found a kind of consolation within the very farewells that ended his hopes.

"Well, she did think of me," he said, wiping his eyes. We all agreed quickly that we would not rest for an instant before we had discovered some trace of the fugitive.

The grandfather and Cecco left at once to ask about her among the innumerable convents in the town. Beppo and the grandmother rushed off to the homes of all Graziella's young friends, suspecting that some of them might have been given some hints about her plans and her flight. As for me, the stranger, I decided to set off for the quays and the ports of Naples as well as the city gates to question the guards, the ship captains, the sailors, and find out if any of them might have seen a young Procidan girl leave the town and get on board a boat.

The morning was spent in vain searches. We all returned to the house silent and depressed to tell each other about our procedures and to consult together. No one, except for the children, had the strength to carry a piece of bread to our lips. Andrea and his wife sat disconsolately in the doorway to Graziella's room. Beppino and Cecco went off to wander, though without any hope, through the streets and the churches, which open in the evenings in Naples for litanies and benedictions.

XV

I went off alone after they had gone, and simply by chance I took the path that led to the grotto of Pausilippo. I went through the grotto and came to the shore of the sea that bathes the little island of Nisida.

From the shore, I let my gaze wander toward Procida, which from there appeared bright, like a tortoise shell on the blue waves. My thoughts followed naturally, and I remembered that island and the holidays I had spent there with Graziella. I felt a sudden inspiration to go there. I remembered that she had a friend there, about my age, the daughter of a poor inhabitant of one of the neighboring houses, and that this girl wore clothing that was unlike that of her companions. One day I asked her about this difference in their clothes and she told me that she was a nun, though she lived freely with her parents in a kind of intermediate state between the church and her convent. She showed me the church to which her convent belonged. There were several on the island, as well as on Ischia and in the villages throughout the countryside around Naples.

The idea occurred to me that Graziella, wanting to devote herself to God, might perhaps come and confide in her friend and ask her to open the gates of her convent. Without taking any further time to reflect on the idea, I walked off swiftly in the direction of Pozzuoli, the town closest to Procida where one could find a boat.

I was in Pozzuoli in less than an hour. I hurried to the port; I paid two men double to get me to Procida, despite the rough sea and the coming nightfall. They got their boat in the water. I picked up a pair of oars and rowed with them. We reached the cape of Miseno with difficulty. Two hours later we landed on the island, and alone I clambered out of the boat, out of breath and shivering, in the darkness and the winter wind, and ascended the long ramp that led up to the cabin of Andrea.

XVI

"If Graziella is on the island," I said to myself, "she would have come here first, with that same instinct that directs the bird to her nest and the child to the home of his father. If she's not in the cabin now, there should be some traces to tell me whether she had been. And maybe those traces can be clues to guide me to wherever she is. If I don't find her or any traces, everything is lost: then the gates of some living sepulchre will have closed upon her youth."

Disturbed by that terrible fear, I climbed up to the very top step. I knew the little niche in the rock face where the old grandmother had left the key when she departed. I pulled aside the ivy and plunged my hand inside. My fingertips groped for the key, half-frozen with the fear of finding it, of feeling the cold iron, which would mean there was no hope left . . .

The key was not there. I just stifled a cry of joy, and I stole silently into the courtyard. The door and shutters were closed; a faint light escaped from the window, floating out on the fig leaves and betraying the presence of a lamp within. Who could have found the key, opened the door, and lit the lamp if not the child of the house? I was certain that Graziella was only a few steps away from me, and I fell silently to my knees there on the last step to thank the angel who had guided me to her.

XVII

The house was utterly silent. Pressing my ear to the door, I thought I could make out a thin sound, like breathing or perhaps weeping, coming from the inner room. I opened the door carefully, making it tremble slightly as if the wind were moving it on its hinges, in order to attract Graziella's attention delicately, in case the sudden sound of a human voice would be the death of her. The breathing sound stopped. Then I called her name, half-aloud but in the calmest and tenderest manner I could. A feeble cry was the response, coming from the very back of the house.

I called her name again, asking her to open the door

for her friend, for her brother who had come alone, at night, through the tempest, guided by his guardian angel to seek for her, to find her, to help her out of her despair, and to bring her the forgiveness of her family, and to return her to her duties, her happiness, her poor grandmother, and her two dear little children!

"God! It's him! Calling my name—his voice!" she exclaimed in a stifled voice.

Then, even more tenderly, I called her Graziellina, that name that is a kind of caress, the name I sometimes called her when we were laughing together.

"Oh, it really is him," she said. "I'm not imagining it, my God! It really is him!"

I could hear her getting up and rustling the dry leaves on the floor as she moved, coming toward the door to open it, then falling back again out of weakness or emotion, without the strength to come any farther.

XVIII

I no longer hesitated: I pushed the door open with my shoulder with all the strength that my impatience and anxiety gave me, and the latch snapped and gave, and I rushed into the first room.

The little lamp Graziella had lit in front of the Madonna now cast a faint light. I hurried to the back of the second room where I had heard her voice and what I thought was the sound of her fainting. She didn't seem to be there. But her weakness betrayed her: she had fallen back upon the pile of dry heather that served as her bed, and now she stared at me, her hands clasped together. Her eyes were lit up by fever, wide open with surprise, and languid with love; she fixed those bright eyes upon me like the light of two stars that, from their height in the heavens, seem to gaze down directly upon you.

She tried to raise her head, but it sank back feebly

against the bed of leaves; it was twisted toward me, as if her neck had been broken. She was as pale as death, except where the tint of living roses blushed on her cheekbones. Her beautiful skin was mottled where dust had settled in on her teardrops. Her black dress seemed to meld in with the dark brown of the leaves spread all over the floor and on her bed. Her bare feet, white as marble, stretched out beyond the leaves and ferns, resting on the stone floor. The cold ran through her limbs, making them shiver and making her teeth clatter like castanets in the hands of a child. The red kerchief that usually covered her beautiful long black hair was in disarray and hung down over her forehead almost like a half-veil. I saw that she had used it to hide her face and her tears in the darkness, like the shroud in which she expected soon to be covered, and that she had only pushed it up and off her face when she had heard my voice and got up to open the door for me.

XIX

I rushed to her and knelt beside the bed of heather; I took her two icy hands in mine; I brought them to my lips to warm them with my breath; some of my teardrops fell on them. I understood from the convulsive way in which she pressed my fingers that she had felt the drops and knew they came from my heart, and that she was thanking me. I pulled off my mariner's cap and used it to cover her bare feet, wrapping them in the folds of its wool.

She let me do it, following me with her eyes, and with an expression of delirious happiness, but without the strength to move in any way to help me, like a child who lets herself be wrapped up in a blanket and returned to the cradle. Then I threw two or three bundles of heather onto the fireplace in the first room to warm the air a bit. I lit them with the lamp's flame, and then I returned to sit down on the floor next to the bed of leaves.

"I feel so much better!" she said in a low voice, smooth and flat, as if her lungs were too weak to allow her to put any variation or expression into her words. "I tried, in vain, to hide it from myself, and I wanted to hide it from you forever, from you especially. I can die, but I can't love anyone other than you. They want to give me a fiancé, but you are the fiancé of my soul! I will not give myself to anyone else on this earth, because I have already given myself in secret to you! Only you on this earth, or God in heaven—that's the vow I made on the first day I realized my heart was sick for you. I know very well that I'm nothing but a poor girl and I'm not worthy to touch your feet, even in thought. So I never asked to be loved in return. I will never ask you if you love me. But I love you—I love you—I love you!" She seemed to concentrate her whole soul in those three words. "And now, despise me, mock me, trample me under your feet! Laugh at me, if you want to, the way you would at some madwoman dressed in rags who thinks she's the queen. Expose me to the ridicule of the whole world. And if you do, I will say to them all: 'Yes, I love him! And if you had been in my place, you would have done just the same; you would either die or love him!'"

XX

I kept my eyes lowered, not daring to look up at her, for fear that my face would say either too much or too little to her in her delirium. But at those last words I raised my forehead, which had been pressed against her hands, and I stammered a few words.

She put her finger against my lips. "No, let me say everything: right now, I am happy; I have no more doubts; God has explained Himself. Listen:

"Yesterday, when I escaped from the house after a night spent in misery, weeping at your door, when I came through a tempest to get here, I arrived sure that I would never see you again; I was like a dead woman, walking toward her tomb. My plan was to join the convent the next day, as soon as dawn came. But when I got to the island at night and I went to knock at the convent gate, it was too late, and the gates were locked. They would not let me in. I came here to spend the night and to kiss the walls of my father's house before entering the house of God and the tomb of my heart. I had a child send a note to my friend to come and get me tomorrow. I took the key. I lit the lamp in front of the Madonna. I got down on my knees and I made a vow, a final vow, a vow of hope from the heart of despair. Because you will learn this, if you ever love, that there is always an ember of hope in the depths of the soul, even when you think the flames are entirely extinguished. 'Holy Mother,' I said to her, 'send me a sign of my vocation, to assure me that love is not tricking me and that I am truly giving my life up to God, a life that should belong entirely to Him!

"'And this is how it begins, my last night among the living. No one will know where I spent it. Perhaps tomorrow they will come and look for me here, but I will be gone. If the friend I wrote to is the first one to come, that will be the sign that I must carry out my plan, and I will follow her to the convent, forever.

"'But if *he* comes, before her! If he comes, guided by my guardian angel, to find me and stop me from crossing the border between two lives! . . . Oh, then that will be a sign that you do not want me and that I should return with him, to love him for the rest of my days!

"'Do what you will with me,' I told her. 'Do this one additional miracle, if it is your will and God's! And for that miracle I will give you a gift, the only one I can give you, for I have nothing. Here is my hair, my poor, long hair that he likes and that he has toyed with so often, laughing to see the wind blow it around my shoulders. Take it, I give it to you; I will cut it myself, to prove to you that I'm keeping nothing back and that my head submits to the scissors now, before tomorrow, when they will cut it off to separate me forever from the world.'"

At these words, she raised her left hand and swept off the red silk kerchief, and with her other hand picking up the long sheaf of hair that lay beside her on the bed of leaves, she unrolled it and showed it to me. "The Madonna has done the miracle!" she exclaimed, her voice stronger now and accented with joy. "She has sent you to me! I will go wherever you wish, wherever you go. My hair is for her. My life is for you!"

I buried my face in that beautiful black hair, holding it in my hands like a dead branch cut from a tree. I silently covered it with kisses, pressed it against my heart, wet it with tears as if it were some part of herself that was dead and that I was burying in the ground. Then, looking up at her, I saw her beautiful head despoiled and yet somehow seeming adorned and embellished by her sacrifice, and now radiant with joy and love even amid the uneven, ruined stumps of black hair on her scalp, where the hair had been torn off rather than cut by the scissors. I thought she looked like a mutilated statue of Youth, upon which the very mutilations wrought by Time only served to bring out the work's grace and beauty, making the viewer feel a more tender admiration. This profanation of herself, the suicide of her beauty born out of her love for me, gave me such a shock that I felt overwhelmed, and I bowed my head down at her feet. I truly felt what it is to love, and I took that feeling for love!

XXI

But alas, it was not real, complete love; it was only the shadow of love within me. And I was so young and so naive that I couldn't help fooling myself. I believed that I adored her in the way that such innocence, beauty, and love deserved to be adored by a lover. I said as much to her in that emotional tone of voice that passion gives us, when aided by solitude, the night, despair, and tears. She believed it, because she needed to believe it in order to go on living, and because she had enough passion within herself to make up for its absence in a thousand other hearts.

The whole night passed thus in intimate conversation—intimate, but naive and pure—between two creatures who innocently reveal their tender feelings, two creatures who wish the night and the silence were eternal, so that nothing else could ever come and interpose itself between the tongue and the heart. There was no moral danger: her piety and my own timid reserve saw to that. The veil of our tears maintained our chastity. Nothing is more foreign to sensuality than tenderness. To abuse such an intimacy would be to profane two souls.[2]

I held her two hands in mine. I could feel the life returning to them. I went to find water for her, both to drink and to bathe her face, and I brought it back cupped in the palms of my hands. I restarted the fire by throwing in some branches; then I returned, sitting down on the stone next to the heap of myrtle branches that still cushioned her head, in order to listen, and listen again, to her delicious avowals of love: how it was born within her unbeknownst to her, seeming to be only a pure, sweet sisterly affection; how she was alarmed at first, but then reassured herself; what the first sign was that told her it was love; how many secret marks of her love she had shown me, without my realizing it; what that day was like when she felt she had betrayed herself; what that other day was like when she thought I loved her too; the hours, the gestures, the smiles, the little words that escaped her lips and then were taken back, the revelations, the involuntary clouding over of our faces during these past six months . . . . She had retained it all within her memory; she remembered it all, the way the grass on the mountainsides in the Midi remembers: the heat of the summer sun sets it ablaze, but long after, traces always remain, everywhere that the flames have passed.

XXII

She told me also about some of those mysterious little superstitions to which love is prone, which assign meaning and importance to the most insignificant circumstances. It was as if she were lifting up one by one each of her soul's veils before me. She revealed herself to me as she would to God, in all the nudity of her unhesitating candor and youth. Only once in a lifetime does a soul pour itself out so completely to another soul, with that unstoppable murmur of the lips, lips that cannot keep up with the effusion of love, lips that end in stammering out inarticulate, confused sounds, like the kisses of a little child falling into sleep.

I did not hesitate to listen, to make my own inarticulate responses, to shudder in my turn. And although my own heart was too light, too green with youth, not ripe or fecund enough yet to produce feelings that burned like hers, her emotions, slipping as it were into mine, created an impression so new, so delicious, that in feeling them I believed they were my own. What an error! I was the mirror; she was the flame. In reflecting, I believed I was producing. But no matter; that radiance, echoing back and forth from one to the other, seemed to belong to us both, and we were enveloped in the atmosphere of the same feeling.

XXIII

And so we spent that long winter night. It seemed no longer to her or to me than the time it took to sigh the first sigh of love. And when dawn came, it seemed to interrupt a conversation that had barely begun.

But the sun was high on the horizon when its rays slipped in between the slits of the closed shutters, making the lamp's glow pale. When I opened the door, I saw the whole family of the fisherman outside below, making their way up the stairs.

Graziella's friend, the young nun, to whom she had sent her message the night before, revealing her plan to enter the convent the following day, suspected some sorrow was afflicting her friend's heart, so she sent one of her brothers that night to Naples to inform the family of Graziella's resolution. Knowing now where they would find their child, they made haste to the island, all of them joyous and all of them penitent, hoping to stop her from giving in to her despair and to bring her home with them, free and pardoned.

The grandmother threw herself on her knees next to the bed, pushing forward the two little ones she had brought along to soften Graziella's heart and using them as a kind of shield against the reproaches of her granddaughter. The children rushed forward, crying out and weeping, into the arms of their sister. As Graziella sat up to caress them and to embrace her grandmother, the kerchief covering her head slipped off, revealing her bare scalp, shorn of her hair. At the sight of such an outrage upon her beauty, the meaning of which they understood at once, they trembled. Sobbing broke out anew throughout the house.

The young nun calmed and consoled them; she gathered up Graziella's cut hair, touched it to the Madonna statue, and then tied it up in a white silk kerchief, placing it in the grandmother's apron, spread across her lap.

"Keep this," she said, "and show it to her from time to time, both in her times of happiness and sorrow, to remind her, whenever she finds the man she is going to love, that the first fruits of her heart must always belong to God, just as these first fruits of her beauty belong to Him."

XXIV

That evening we all returned to Naples. The zeal I had shown in finding and rescuing Graziella in the situation had redoubled the affection the old fisherman and his wife felt for me. Neither of them suspected the nature of my interest in her or her attachment to me. They attributed everything to the deformity and appearance of Cecco. They hoped she would overcome that repugnance with reason and with time. They promised to stop pressuring Graziella about the marriage. Cecco himself begged his father to stop speaking to them about it; and in his own humility of character and appearance, he begged his cousin's pardon for having been the cause of so much pain. Calm descended again upon the household.

XXV

No more clouds darkened Graziella's expression or my happiness, apart from the thought that this happiness sooner or later must be interrupted by my return to my own country. When anyone made any reference to France, the poor girl went pale, as if she had seen the angel of Death. One day I returned to my room to find all my city clothes torn up and scattered on the floor. "Forgive me," said Graziella, falling to her knees before me and gazing up at me with an anxious, disturbed expression on her face. "I'm responsible for this wickedness. But oh, please don't scold me! Everything that reminds me that you will have to change from your fisherman's clothes is just too painful for me! It's as if you will remove me from your heart and put another in my place, when you put the clothes back on you used to wear!"

Apart from these little outbursts, which arose only out of the heat of her tenderness and were quickly soothed by our tears, three months passed in an imaginary happiness that the slightest intrusion of reality would have destroyed at once. Our Eden was built upon a mere cloud.

And so it was that I learned about love: from some tears in the eyes of a child.

XXVI

We were so happy when we could completely forget that any other world beyond ours existed, any world beyond that little house on a hillside in Pausilippo; that terrace in the sunlight, that little room where we worked or, rather, played half the day; that boat, safely laid in its bed of sand on the beach, and that beautiful sea whose humid, sonorous winds carried the cool melodies of the sea to our ears.

But alas, there were moments when we were forced to recognize that the world was not bounded by Naples and that a day would come when we were no longer together under the light of the same sun or moon. I am wrong to indict my heart for dryness then by comparing it with what I have felt since. In the depths of my heart, I was in truth beginning to love Graziella a thousand times more than I admitted to myself. If I had not loved her so much, the trace she left in my soul for my whole life would not be so deeply etched, or so sorrowful, and the memory of her would not be so delightful and so sad, and her image would not remain so vivid and so striking in my memory. My heart may have been sandy soil in those days, but that sea flower took root there for more than a mere season, like those miraculous lilies that live and blossom on the shores of the isle of Ischia.

XXVII

And what eye so deprived of light, what heart so dead that it would not have loved her? Her beauty seemed to grow and increase from evening to morning, along with her love. Her body was full-grown, but her grace increased in every way: the child's graces of yesterday had become the flowering graces of a young woman today. Her svelte child's body visibly evolved, taking on the smooth, rounded contours of young adulthood. She seemed more solid now, but without losing any of her suppleness. Her bare feet no longer tripped so lightly over the hard soil. Now she would trail them indolently, languorously, with the kind of languor that seems to imprint itself upon the bodies of women when their thoughts first turn to love.

Her hair grew back, thick and full, like the sea plants that grow thick in the warm tides of springtime. I would sometimes amuse myself by measuring it, twining it around my fingers and holding it against the braid of her green vest. Her skin seemed to grow whiter and rosier at the same time, with that same tint that the pink coral dust left on her fingers every day. Her eyes seemed to grow larger and seemed to be opening every day on a horizon she had never seen before. It was an astonishment at being alive, the same astonishment that Galatea felt when she first felt life begin to palpitate within the marble. She evinced some little modesties and timidities with me that she had never shown before, little glances and gestures she had never made before. I observed it all, and I was sometimes struck mute and even trembled around her. We may have looked like two guilty creatures, but we were only a pair of children who were too happy.

And yet for some time a stratum of sadness was hiding, and sometimes revealed itself, under that happiness. We did not really understand it. But fate knew it very well. It was the feeling of how short the time was that remained of our life together.

XXVIII

Often Graziella, instead of happily taking up her work again after washing and dressing her little brothers, would remain sitting outside, leaning against the terrace wall, in the shade of the big leaves of the fig tree that grew all the way from the ground below up over the top of the wall. She would sit there motionless, gazing off into the distance, for half the day sometimes. When her grandmother would ask if she felt ill, she would reply that there was nothing wrong with her, but she already felt tired, even before beginning her work. At times like those, she did not like to be questioned. She would turn away from everyone, except me. But then she would look at me for a long time without saying anything. Sometimes her lips moved slightly as if she were speaking, but she was muttering words no one could hear. I could see little shivers, sometimes pink and sometimes white, running over the skin of her cheeks, wrinkling subtly, like the surface of the sea when it is touched by the first hints of the morning breezes. But when I would come and sit down beside her and gently tickle the long lashes of her closed eyes with the feather of my pen, or with a twig from the rosemary bush—then she would forget everything, and she would begin to laugh and to chatter with me as she normally did. But sometimes after the laughing and joking she would grow sad again.

I would ask her sometimes, "Graziella, what is it you're looking at out there on the sea? What is it you stare at for hours? Do you see something that we don't see?"

"I see France, standing behind mountains of ice," she would reply.

"And what is it that's so beautiful in France?" I would continue.

"I see someone who looks like you," she would say, "someone walking, walking, walking along a white road that never ends. He walks without ever turning around, ever, always looking ahead, and I wait for hours on end, always hoping he will turn and walk back. But he never turns!" At that, she buried her face in her apron, and no matter how many tender names I called her, she would not raise her head.

Then I would sadly go to my room. I would try reading to distract myself, but I would always see her face between me and the page. It would seem as if the words on the page took on a voice, and that they were sighing, the way our hearts did. Often, I would end by weeping there alone, but I was ashamed of my melancholy, and I never told Graziella that I had wept. Oh, how wrong I was: how much good one tear of mine would have done!

XXIX

I remember the incident that gave her the most pain, one from which she never recovered completely.

She had a long-standing friendship with two or three girls who were about her age. These girls lived in one of the cottages in the nearby gardens. They ironed and mended dresses for a boarding school for young French girls. Murat, the king, had established this school in Naples for the daughters of his ministers and generals.[3] The young Procidan girls often talked with Graziella as they did their work; she would watch them over the wall on the terrace. They showed her the fine lace, the beautiful silks, hats, slippers, ribbons, scarves—all the items they brought from the boarding school and returned to it. The cries of astonishment and admiration were endless. Sometimes the young workers would come and take Graziella with them to Mass or the vespers service with music in the little chapel of Pausilippo. I would go to meet them when evening was falling and the repeated tinkling of the bells told me that the priest was nearing the benediction. We would return, romping along the seaside, rushing forward when the wave retreated, and retreating when the swell of a wave came toward us, ending in foam at our feet. God, how lovely Graziella was then! She would run away, fearful of getting her good slippers wet, the ones embroidered with gold thread, her arms stretched out in front of her, toward me as if she would take refuge on my breast from the pursuit of the envious wave that always tried to catch hold of her, or at least kiss her feet!

XXX

I saw that she had been keeping some scheme of hers secret from me for some time. She had been having whispered conversations with her young friends, the workers. Apparently there was some little plot afoot, which excluded me.

One evening I was reading in my room, by the light of a little earthenware lamp. My door onto the terrace was open to let in the sea breeze. I heard some sounds in the room where Graziella and the children slept—girls whispering, stifled laughter, then little exclamations, then new outbursts of chatter interrupted by long silences. At first, I paid it no attention.

But then the very effort they put into stifling their

whispered voices and the mystery it all suggested excited my curiosity. I set my book down, and taking my lamp in my left hand, I cupped it with my right to prevent the breeze from extinguishing it. I moved on tiptoe across the terrace, stepping quietly on the stones. I pressed my ear up close against Graziella's door. I could hear footsteps going back and forth inside the room, and the rustlings of material being folded and refolded, the clicking of thimbles, pins, and scissors as women were adjusting ribbons and pinning up scarves, and along with it the kind of murmuring and buzzing of young voices that I had often heard in my mother's house when my sisters were getting dressed for a ball.

But there was certainly no ball planned in Pausilippo for the next day. And Graziella never so much as dreamed of enhancing her beauty by her clothes or hairdo. There was not even a mirror in her room. When she wanted to look at herself, she gazed into the well on the terrace—or, rather, the only times she really looked at herself were when she gazed into my eyes.

This mystery was too much for my curiosity. I pushed the door with my knee and it opened. There I was, lamp in hand, on the threshold.

The young workers all emitted a cry of alarm and scattered like a flock of birds, hiding themselves in the corners of the room as if they had been surprised in the middle of some criminal act. They were still holding the objects that would prove them guilty—one the thread, another the scissors, this one some flowers, that one some ribbons. But Graziella, sitting in the middle of the room on a little wooden stool, petrified by my sudden entrance, could not escape. She was as red as a pomegranate. She lowered her eyes, not daring to meet my gaze, barely breathing. Everyone in the room was silent, all waiting to hear what I was going to say. I said nothing. I was too absorbed in my surprise and in mute contemplation of what I saw.

Graziella had taken off her heavy wool clothes; she had removed the typically Procidan over-vest trimmed with braid, open in the front so that a young girl can breathe and so that a mother can nurse a child; her slippers with their gold spangles and their wooden heels, normally worn over bare feet; those long hairpins with little brass balls on their ends, around which she would roll her black hair, like a sail wrapped around a yardarm. And her earrings, large as bracelets, had been thrown on the bed haphazardly, along with her ordinary clothes.

Instead of that picturesque Greek-influenced costume that suited a poor girl just as well as a rich one—with its skirt falling halfway down the calf, its blouse with its V-shaped neckline and flowing sleeves, that costume that allowed for the perfect freedom of the body—instead of this, Graziella's young friends had dressed her, at her entreaty, in the dress and ornaments of a French mademoiselle from the convent school who would be about her age and size. She wore a dress of shimmering silk, a pink belt, a white scarf, hair decorated with artificial flowers, slippers of blue satin, and thin silk stockings that showed the color of her skin at her rounded ankles.

She sat there, wearing that costume in which I had just surprised her, as confounded as if she had been surprised in the nude by a man's gaze. I stared at her, unable to tear my eyes away, but without making any gesture or any exclamation or even a smile, which would have given her the impression that I approved of this disguise. I felt tears rising up in my heart. I had suddenly, and all too well, understood the poor girl's thinking. Ashamed of the difference in her and my social rank, she had wanted to see if a change of clothing would reduce that difference, if it would help me see our two destinies as joined. She had tried this without my knowing about it, with the help of her friends, hoping she would then appear before me suddenly more beautiful and more suited to me than she felt in her native dress. But she was so wrong. She could tell by my silence. Her face took on an expression of desperate impatience, almost as if she were going to burst into tears, and at once I understood her secret scheme, her crime, and her disappointment.

In fact, she was very beautiful. Her plan should have embellished her beauty a thousand times in my eyes. But that beauty looked somehow like a kind of torture. It was like one of those young virgins painted by Correggio, nailed to a stake in martyrdom, twisting in their bonds in an attempt to escape from the stares that were a profanation of their chastity. Oh, and indeed it was a martyrdom for poor Graziella! But it was not, as an observer might have thought, the martyrdom of her vanity. No: it was the martyrdom of her love.

The clothes of the young French boarding-school girl had been tailored, no doubt, for a thinner body, for the spindly arms and shoulders of a cloistered child of thirteen or fourteen, and they were too tight for the fully developed figure, the strong, rounded shoulders of this beautiful creature of the sun and the sea. The dress puckered out in places, across her shoulders, across her breast, around the belt, like the bark on a sycamore branch in the spring, when the rising sap cracks it and splits it open. In vain her young helpers had tried to pin up both the dress and the scarf here and there, but nature had undone their work with every movement Graziella made. In several places, where the silk was stretched too taut, her bare neck and arms showed through. The rough cotton of her undergarment showed through, too, contrasting with the elegance of the silk dress. Her arms, encased in too-small and too-tight sleeves, protruded like a pink butterfly pushing out from and bursting its chrysalis. Her feet, accustomed to being bare or wearing loose Greek slippers, swelled the satin of these slippers; her feet seemed imprisoned in their tightly drawn straps, making them look like sandals on her. Her hair, poorly restrained in the network of lace and fake flowers, of its own power raised up the coiffure structure, and while the result was charming—despite all the efforts to disfigure her—all that ornament gave an overly bold, almost immodest appearance to her face, creating a strange and yet erotic contrast.

Her posture seemed as embarrassed as her facial expression. She dared not make a single movement, for fear of letting the flowers fall down from her hair or of marring the dress. She could not walk, for those shoes encased her feet so tightly that her steps would have been awkward. It was as if this naive, innocent Eve of the sea and sun had been suddenly surprised, trapped in her first attempt at coquetry.

XXXI

The silence in the room lasted another minute or so. Finally, more annoyed than pleased by this profanation of nature, I walked toward her making a slightly mocking face, looking her over with a gentle tone of reproach, a friendly kind of teasing, pretending to be unable to recognize her under all that complicated costumery.

"What!" I exclaimed. "Is that you, Graziella? Oh, who would have ever recognized the beautiful Procida girl in this Parisian doll? Come on now," I went on, a little rudely. "Aren't you ashamed of disfiguring what God created to be so charming in her natural dress? You're wasting your time! You'll never be anything but a daughter of the waves, and your hair will always be arranged by the winds of your beautiful sky. These clothes are meant for a bird in a cage, not for a swallow of the seas."

This pierced her to the heart. She did not understand that I preferred the sea swallow—preferred it passionately, adoringly. She thought that I was telling her she should never try to look like someone of my race and my country. She thought that all the efforts she had undertaken to make herself look more beautiful to me, to trick me into thinking she was something else, had been in vain. She abruptly burst into tears and went to sit on her bed; she covered her face with her fingers, and in a sullen tone she asked her friends to help her get that odious costume off.

"I know very well," she said with a sigh, "that I'm nothing but a poor Procida girl. But I thought that by changing my appearance I would not cause you quite so much shame if I ever were to come to your country. But now I see that I have to stay here and die in the place where I was born. But you didn't have to scold me like that."

With that, she ripped off, with contempt, the flowers, the bonnet, the scarf, and angrily throwing them away from her as far as she could, she went over and ground them under her feet, muttering angry words of reproach to them, just as her grandmother had done with the planks of the boat after our shipwreck. Then she rushed over to me and blew out the flame of the lamp I was holding so that I would be unable to see her any longer in the costume that displeased me.

I felt how wrong I had been to tease her so rudely, and I now saw how seriously she took it. I asked her to forgive me. I told her that I had only teased her because I found her a thousand times more attractive as a Procidan than as a French girl. And that was true. But the blow had landed. She wasn't listening to me; she was sobbing.

Her friends helped her undress; I did not see her again until the morning. She now wore her island dress. But her eyes were red with the tears that my teasing had cost her all night long.

XXXII

Around this same time, she began to be worried about letters I received from France, suspecting that one of those letters would be calling me back. She dared not keep them from me, for she was too honest and could not be deceptive even to save her life. But sometimes she held onto them for nine days at a time, keeping them pinned up, with her little golden hairpins, behind the image of the Madonna that hung beside her bed. She thought that the Blessed Virgin would be attracted by these novenas and, looking kindly on our love, would miraculously change the contents of the letters, transforming the command to return into an invitation to remain here with her. None of these little pious frauds escaped me, and they all endeared her to me even more. But the time was approaching.

XXXIII

One evening toward the end of the month of May, there was a loud knocking at the door. The whole family was asleep. I went to answer. It was my old friend V***.[4]

"I've come to find you," he said. "Here's a letter from your mother. You must obey her. We have horses ready at midnight, and it's eleven now. Come away now, or you never will. And that would kill your mother. You know how the family always holds her responsible for your faults. She has sacrificed so much for you; come, sacrifice a little for her. I promise that I'll come back with you, and we can spend another winter and even another year here. But you really must make an appearance at home and show that you do obey your mother."

I was lost; I knew it.

"Wait here for me," I said.

I went back into my room and hurriedly threw my clothes into my suitcase. I wrote a note to Graziella, saying everything that the passion of an eighteen-year-old heart could say, and everything that the rational thinking of a son devoted to his mother could say. I promised her—and I promised myself too—that I would be back within four months and that I would never leave her again after that. I entrusted our future to Providence and to love. I left her my money to help her old grandparents during my absence. I folded the letter and tiptoed to her room. I knelt down at her threshold. I kissed the wood of the door and the stone of the lintel; I slipped the note under the door and into her room. I swallowed the tears that were welling up inside me.

My friend put his hand under my arm and lifted me up, pulling me away with him. And at that same moment Graziella, alarmed no doubt by the unusual sounds outside her door, flung the door open. The terrace was bright in the moonlight. The poor girl recognized my friend. She saw my suitcase, which a hired servant was carrying on his shoulders. She held her arms out toward me, emitted a cry of terror, and fainted, falling down on the terrace.

We rushed toward her and carried her, still unconscious, back to her bed. The whole family was awake now, and they all ran in. Someone splashed some water into her face. All the voices dearest to her were calling to her. But she only regained consciousness when she heard my voice.

"Look," said my friend to me, "she is fine; she has absorbed the blow. Long goodbyes will only give her even more pain." He removed the girl's cold arms from around my neck and pulled me with him out of the house. An hour later, we were in a carriage, rolling in the silence of the night along the road to Rome.

XXXIV

In the letter I left Graziella, I had listed a number of addresses along my route home. I had my first letter from her in Milan. She said that she was physically well but sick at heart; but, she added, she would trust in my word and would wait with confidence for me to return in November.

When I arrived in Lyon, I had a second letter from her, this one calmer and even more confident. The letter included several petals from the red carnation that grew in an earthenware vase on the terrace wall, quite close to my room; she took a flower from that pot every Sunday and wore it in her hair. Did she send me those because she wanted me to have something she had touched? Was it a gentle reproach hidden beneath a symbol, a reminder that she had sacrificed her hair for me?

She told me that she had had a fever; that her heart had been giving her pain; but that she was getting a little better every day; and that in order to give her a change of air, they had sent her to visit one of the family's cousins, a sister to Cecco, who lived in a house in Vomero, up on a high hillside where the air was healthful, overlooking Naples.

Then three months passed without my receiving another letter. I thought about Graziella every day. I planned to depart for Italy toward the beginning of the winter. Her image, sorrowful and charming, appeared in my mind's eye like a regret, and sometimes also like a rebuke. I was at that unappreciative age, when levity combines with the desire to be like others to make a young man ashamed of his very finest feelings; a cruel age, when the finest gifts God gives us—pure love, innocent affection—tumble from our hands into the sand, where the winds of the world pick them up in their bloom and blow them away. My own wicked vanity and my friends' brutal irony waged a kind of war inside me on the hidden tenderness that lived in the depths of my heart. I would not have dared to admit—not without blushing, and not without exposing myself to mockery—the name and the social condition of she who was the object of my regrets and my sorrows. Graziella was not forgotten, but she was now veiled in my life. This love that enchanted my heart also humiliated me. Her memory, which I cherished only when I was in perfect solitude, pursued me now through my dealings with the world like remorse. Oh, how I blush today to remember how I blushed then! And how a single ray of joy or a single tear from her eye was worth more than all the romantic glances, all the flirting, all the smiles for which I was so ready to trade her image! Oh, a young man is incapable of loving! He understands the price of nothing. He only knows real happiness after he has lost it. There is more wild sap, more wavering shade among the young plants of the forest; there is more fire in the old heart of the oak.

Real love is the ripe fruit of life. At eighteen, a boy does not know of it, cannot even imagine it. In the world of vegetation, when the fruit comes, the leaves fall; and so, perhaps, it is in the human world as well. I have often thought so, ever since my hair has begun to go white. I have reproached myself for failing to see the worth of that flower of love. I was vanity, nothing but vanity. Vanity is the stupidest and the cruelest of vices, because it makes us ashamed of our happiness!

XXXV

One evening toward the beginning of November, I had just come back home after a ball, when I received a letter and a package; a traveler from Naples, stopping to change horses in Mâcon, had brought it to me. The unknown traveler's letter told me that a friend of his, the director of a coral work factory in Naples, had charged him with delivering an important message to me, and he had fulfilled his obligation in giving these items to me. But since the news he was bringing would be unhappy and dismal, he would not stay to meet me, instead asking me to send him an acknowledgment of receipt in Paris.

I trembled as I opened the package. Within it, in the first envelope, was the last letter Graziella would write me, containing these words: "The doctor says I will die within a few days. I want to say farewell to you before I lose all my strength. But oh, if you were here, I would live! Still, this is the will of God. I will speak to you soon, and often, from heaven. Love my soul! It will be with you for the rest of your life. I leave you my hair, cut off for you that night. Give it to God, in a chapel in your country, so that something of me will always be near you!"

XXXVI

I sat there, devastated, the letter in my hands, until dawn. Only then did I have the strength to open the second envelope. There it was, all her beautiful hair, just as it was on that night in the cabin when she showed it to me. Some heather leaves that had become attached to it that night were still mixed in. I did as she had requested with her last wish. And the shadow of her death, from that day onward, fell across my face and across my youth.

Twelve years later I returned to Naples. I sought out some trace of her. I found nothing, either on Margellina or Procida. The little house on the island's beach had fallen to ruin. It was nothing now but a pile of gray rocks, forming a shelter for the goatherds and their goats during the rainstorms. Time erases things on earth quickly, but it never erases the trace of a first love in the heart where it once lived.

Poor Graziella! So many days have passed since then. I have been in love, and I have been loved. My road has been illuminated by the radiance of other beauties, other tendernesses. Other women's hearts have opened to me, revealing the most mysterious treasures of beauty, holiness, purity to which God has given life on this earth in order to make us understand, foresee, and desire heaven. But Graziella, nothing has tarnished your image, the first one in my heart. The longer I live, the closer I draw to you in my thoughts. Your memory is like the fire of your grandfather's burning boat, and as it recedes so does the smoke, but the light it gives off seems to intensify; it recedes further and further from us, but the glow only grows brighter. I don't know where your mortal remains are laid to rest, or if anyone mourns you in your native land; but your true sepulchre is in my soul. There you are taken in, and there you are buried. Never will I hear your name in vain. I love the language in which that name is pronounced. In the deepest recess of my heart, there is a tear that drops secretly and keeps on dropping, watering and refreshing your memory, embalming it deep within me.

1829[5]

XXXVII

One evening in the year 1830, having stopped inside a church in Paris, I saw people carrying the casket, draped with a white cloth, of a young girl.[6] The casket made me think of Graziella. I hid myself behind a pillar, in the shadows. I recalled Procida, and I wept for a long while.

My tears eventually stopped, but the clouds that overcast my thoughts during that sad burial service did not dissipate. I returned to my room in silence. I went back over the memories that I have recounted in this long note, and then, in a single rush and weeping again the whole time, I wrote some verses titled "The First Regret." The poem is a feeble echo, at twenty years' distance, of a feeling that caused the springs of my heart to overflow for the first time. The emotion still lingers, like an inner nerve fiber that was injured long ago and has never really healed.

Here are the verses, balm for a wound, the morning dew of a heart, the scent of a funereal flower. All that is missing is the name Graziella. I would insert it into a stanza if there were, here below, a crystal pure enough to hold this tear, this memory, this name.

THE FIRST REGRET

On the sonorous shore, where the sea of Sorrento
Rolls its blue waves to the base of the orange trees,
You can find, near the path by the sweet-scented
    hedge,
A little flat stone, narrow and thin, lying
Beneath the hurried traveler's steps.

The clover hides a single name beneath its leaves,
A name no echo ever repeats.
But sometimes a passerby stops,
Pushes back the leaves, reads the age and date,
And feeling a tear start in his eye, exclaims:
"Only sixteen! Too young to die!"

> But why dwell on scenes from the past?
> Let the winds howl, let the sea moan;
> Return, return, my sorrowful thoughts!
> I want to dream today, not weep.

"Only sixteen!"—Yes, sixteen years, and never
Did sixteen bloom upon a finer face, never

Were seething waves reflected in purer eye!
I, only I, see her now; my thought brings her
Back, up from the soul, where nothing dies,
Alive again! As she was when her eyes were
On mine, the first time we talked, on the sea;
The winds unfurled that black hair, took it,
The sail's shadow grazed her cheek, and
She listened to the fishermen's nocturne,
Carried toward us on the air, cool, fresh,
And she showed me above where the moon grew
Like a flower of night, shy of the dawn, and
The silver-foaming waves, and said to me:
"Why does everything gleam so, in the air
And within me? Never before were those
Azure fields sown with so many lights; those
Golden sands where the waves go to die, those
Mountain peaks that tremble in the sky, those
Coastlines crowned with silent trees, those
Lights on the coast, and those songs on the waves,
Never before have they charged me like this,
Enchanted my senses! Why have I never dreamed
Like this before? Is a star rising in my heart?
And you, child of the morning, speak: Are there
Nights like these where you come from? Are they
Like this in places that I've never been?"
Then, gazing on her mother, she sat down with her,
And rested her head on her knees.

> But why dwell on scenes from the past?
> Let the winds howl, let the sea moan;
> Return, return, my sorrowful thoughts!
> I want to dream today, not weep.

The purity of her gaze, candor of her voice:
That gaze could drown me in its light!

Nemi Lake,[7] its surface never wrinkled,
Less transparent, less limpid than her eyes.
In them, you could see her thoughts before she
Did; lowering her eyes concealed nothing.
Everything was innocence, her brow
Never visited by pain, her being all joy.
And that fresh smile, to be ended some day
By sorrow, fluttered always on those half-
Opened lips like a purer rainbow
On a perfect day. No clouds darkened
That splendid face, never dimmed its light.
Her step swayed light, uncertain, like a wave
That cradles the infant day, or suddenly
Runs, just for the sake of running;
Silvery, her voice, limpid and pure like
An echo of her childish soul, music
Of that soul where everything is song,
Rising upward in the living air.

> But why dwell on scenes from the past?
> Let the winds howl, let the sea moan;
> Return, return, my sorrowful thoughts!
> I want to dream today, not weep.

The first image engraved on her heart
Was mine—as the awakening eye's
First sight is the sun—and after that day,
She never looked elsewhere for more;
From the day that she loved me, the whole
World was love! She blent me into her life,
Saw everything inhabiting my soul,
And I became part of that enchanted
World floating before her eyes,
Happiness on earth, hope in heaven.
She thought no more of time or place;

The moment was her whole existence;
Before I came, her life had been without
Memory; now, the future was complete:
Always it would be like this evening!
She trusted in sweet Nature, who smiled
On us, and in the pure prayer she carried
To the altar, where she spread it out
Profusely, like her flowers, her heart
Filled with joy, foreign to tears. And I,
Humble as a child, would follow her there,
As she whispered low: "Pray with me! I can't
See heaven clear unless you're there!"

> But why dwell on scenes from the past?
> Let the winds howl, let the sea moan;
> Return, return, my sorrowful thoughts!
> I want to dream today, not weep.

See, in the basin of this pond, living
Water swells, a lake bound tightly
By its shores; blue, clear, sheltered from the winds,
And from the sun whose heat could someday
Dry it all away. On the surface,
Blanket-smooth, floats a white swan.
He plunges his neck below, but the ripples
Adorn, not disturb, the water-mirror,
Cradling there among the evening stars.
But if he took his flight toward some new home,
Beating the air with his still-wet wings,
The lake's blue sky would darken brown, and
A great plume, snowflake-white, would drift back
    down,
To agitate those still waters: as if the vulture,
Enemy to swan race, had dropped death down,
Scattering feathers over the waves,

So now the brilliant blue enchanted lake,
Is only a pond, sand-muddied water.

And so, when I left her, that pure soul
Shuddered, the light went out, and the flame
Ascended to the skies, never to return.
She did not wait for some second future;
She did not dally with hope or doubt;
She did not dispute the claim pain made
Upon her soul; she drank the cup down
All at once; those very first tears were the
Spring in which her heart drowned.
And as a bird, less pure, less fine than she,
Nestles its head beneath its wing at dark,
She put on the shroud of mute despair,
And slept in it, but long, long before the night!

> But why dwell on scenes from the past?
> Let the winds howl, let the sea moan;
> Return, return, my sorrowful thoughts!
> I want to dream today, not weep.

Fifteen years she has slept on her bed of
Clay, and no one weeps anymore for her now,
And forgetting, that second shroud of the dead,
Has covered the path that leads to the shore;
No one visits anymore this worn old stone,
Nor thinks of it, nor prays about it—except
In my thoughts when I remount the stream
That flows from my youth, and I ask my heart
Where they are, the ones that are no more,
And my eyes scan for those dim dear traces,
And I weep for my star-denuded sky!
She was the first, and the sweet starlight

From those pious, gentle days still
Chases off the shadows in my heart.

> But why dwell on scenes from the past?
> Let the winds howl, let the sea moan;
> Return, return, my sorrowful thoughts!
> I want to dream today, not weep.

A thorny bush, its foliage pale green,
Is all that Nature gave for monument;
Battered by sea winds, scorched by the sun,
Like a desolate regret rooted heart-deep,
It lives in that stone but gives it no shade;
The dust from the pathway whitens its leaves;
It creeps low to the ground, its branches bent down
All gnawed and torn by the herdsman's goats.
A single flower in spring, snowflake white,
Flutters there for a day or two; but the wind's
Endless siege strips it off before its scent
Has time to be strewn—like a life, before
It has time to enchant and beguile the heart.
A solitary bird, gentle and melancholy,
Lights there to sing on the drooping branch.
Oh speak, flower withered too soon by life,
Is there not some land somewhere, someplace
Where everything that dies will live again?

> Return, return to the days long past!
> These sad memories help me to feel.
> Follow, my thoughts, go where goes my soul!
> My heart is full, and I must weep.

And this is how I expiated my hardness of heart, the ingratitude of an eighteen-year-old—with these versified tears.
When I reread them, I cannot help but adore, all over

again, that fresh, cool image that the transparent, plaintive waves of the gulf of Naples will always roll before my eyes. . . . And I cannot relive this without despising myself! But the souls on high forgive. Hers has forgiven me. You too, reader, please forgive me too! For I have wept.

CHRONOLOGY

1790   Alphonse de Lamartine born, October 21.

1811   Affair with Henriette Pommier, leading to his departure, in July, for Italy.
On October 24, his relatives return to France, and Lamartine proceeds to Rome. He arrives in Naples on November 30.

1812   Moves into the home of relative Antoine Dareste de la Chavanne. In April, departs Naples to return home.

1813   Affair with Nina de Pierreclau leads to the birth of their son in March.

1816   Death of Mariantonia Iacomino, May 31.
Lamartine meets Julie Charles at Aix-les-Bains in October.

1817   Death of Julie Charles, December 18.

1820   Publication of *Méditations Poétiques*, March 11.
Lamartine marries the English-born Mary Ann Birch on June 6.

1830   Composition of "Le Premier Regret" toward the end of May.

1833   Elected to the Chambre des Députés.

1841   Death of Aymon de Virieu, April 7.

1844   Trip to Italy with wife and family, including Valentine de Cessiat.
Lamaratine resides on Ischia and begins writing *Confidences* and *Graziella*, August–September.

1847 Publication of *Histoire des Girondins*, March–
      June.
1848 Revolution begins in February. Lamartine is
      named Minister of Foreign Affairs, one of five
      leaders of the new Republic. The first presiden-
      tial election is held December 10; Lamartine
      comes in fourth.
1849 Serial publication of *Confidences* in *La Presse*;
      separate publication of *Raphaël* (both in January).
1852 *Graziella* published separately in book form.
1863 Death of Lamartine's wife, May 21.
1868 Valentine de Cessiat officially has her last name
      changed to Lamartine.
1869 Death of Lamartine, February 28.

APPENDIX

Excerpts from Lamartine's Mémoires inédits, *1790–1815*

Lamartine's *Mémoires inédits, 1790–1815* were published in 1870, a year after his death. They purport to tell what really happened in his early life, especially on the trip to Italy in 1811–12 and the meeting with Graziella. He had begun working on the book in 1865 when he was seventy-five years old but had set it aside. In 1867, he published another memoir-cum-novel, *Antoniella*, using the same name and some of the material from his experiences in 1811. He was returning again and again to this era of his life and continuing to find importance and meaning in it. Should we take the story here, in *Mémoires inédits*, as the final, absolute truth of the matter? Or is it simply another version?

The *Mémoires* begin with his earliest memories of childhood and family. In this excerpt, we begin with the young Lamartine just arrived in Naples, having discovered that his good friend Aymon de Virieu is there also: they run into each other on the stairway in the Hotel Florentin, where Lamartine has come to gamble.

Book IV

III

But my mother's letters, which she had given me to take to our relative, Monsieur de La Chavanne, director of the cigar factory in Naples, made me feel a certain guilt; I had neglected to take them to him.[1] An unconfined freedom had seemed preferable to me—more pleasant. But eventually, one had to get the task done. I asked where the tobacco director lived; it was, they told me, in the noisiest district in the city, by the huge, magnificent monastery of San Pietro Martyr. I went there. It was noon. I climbed up, by way of a long, high stairway with 120 steps, up to the fifth or sixth story, where I found a large garden with arcades leading off on every side. These arcades and the lower stories were occupied by the operation's great barrels, workshops, and the numerous workers at this state-owned enterprise. I took notice of every detail, because this was about to turn into one of those decisive adventures, one that changed the course of my life.

When I got to the top level, I rang at a large door that was the entry point to a long, deep cloister, off which several different doors opened, to both the right and left of the gallery. Some *finestrati*, which occupied the far wall of the cloister, let in a blinding light. Young girls were passing in and out of the doors constantly, carrying I didn't know what in their aprons. I learned later that these were children charged with picking out the tobacco leaves to use for making cigarettes. I was far from the thought that one of these girls would before long become *Graziella*, change her occupation, dominate my destiny, and exert an imperishable influence over my entire life. But that was true; we will see how it all came about. I did not dare tell the story when I wrote the true novel, *Graziella*, in 1847, which enjoyed and still enjoys such popularity, because all readers recognize the true accent of nature in it.[2] I slightly altered some of the opening pages, out of vanity; everything else remained true. Now I will tell the whole story. What follows are the beginnings of *Graziella*.

IV

At the back of the cloister, to the right, I saw a brighter light coming out from one of the doors where domestics were coming and going, carrying tableware and plates out and back; a sound like that of knives and forks could be heard. I realized that I was about to present myself to Monsieur the director at his lunchtime, and it was too late now to retreat. I went in, and they announced my name.

At that, Monsieur de la Chavanne got up, caught sight of me, and opening his arms, cried, "The very image of his mother!" He embraced me with what I learned were his customary warmth and affection and had me sit down on a toile sofa, just below the high window that gave light to the dining room. This had been the drawing room of the Superior of the San Pietro Martyr monastery. There were two other people at the table: one was a female, around twenty or twenty-five years old, whom I learned later was called *Antoniella*. She was good-looking, but not remarkable; her familiarity with Monsieur de la Chavanne suggested a long employment in the house; she was in charge of overseeing many of the girls who worked there making cigars; and the other was a ravishing young woman.

Neither of them took part in the conversation, which centered on my mother and my family. Monsieur de la Chavanne told me he would not tolerate my staying in the hotel in Naples and that he would have a room made up for me, with a view of the sea. He showed me the room: there was a camp bed in it, and a little narrow staircase led up from the bed to the flat roof of the enormous monastery, and the entire horizon was the sea; I could see the island of Capri, the mountains of Sorrento, and Vesuvius. There were walls placed around for shelter from the winds, creating spots where you could have your body in the sun and your head in the shade. I was delighted with this large open area adjoining my little room, and I went back down, promising him that I would return quickly to move in.

Monsieur de la Chavanne, of whom I had heard a great deal from my mother, was somewhere between forty and fifty, and remarkably kind-hearted; his sincere, jovial face inspired affection. He was a big man, with sky-blue eyes, a smiling face, and a graceful mouth, which revealed his character.[3] It was impossible not to like him. He had valiantly served his people in the siege of Lyon by the Convention.[4] The siege had ruined him financially; he moved to Italy. The King of Naples, Murat, had given him the tobacco position because of his family; the position was politically neutral, and it was lucrative. He lived in Naples, a free and happy man. He had left his wife and several children in France, where she was raising them with distinction. She came to visit him from time to time; he loved her, and he was loved by her; the necessity of living separated from her was often bitter to him. He lived in Naples as an exile who seeks to forget that he is one; and he was much admired, in any case, by all the French there as well as the Neapolitans, who knew him only by the services that his position allowed him to do for them. This was his world. A man of fifty, yet always young, always likeable—such was this charming character. He was worthy of esteem, and he liked to be liked, so that, providing you liked him, he would pardon all your faults, or all those that were not intentionally hurtful. As I left him that day, I already felt bonded with him. I promised to return soon to enjoy his hospitality, but there was another, secret, invincible charm already working on me: the idea of seeing again the younger of those two charming persons I had met at his table.

V–VI

As I returned to [*his friend, Aymon de*] Virieu, to tell him that I was about to part from him in order to obey my mother, I passed by the post office. I found there a letter from Mâcon, in an unfamiliar handwriting; I trembled as I read it.

[*The letter was from a representative of the Pommier family, informing him that Henriette, the beloved he had left behind, had received an offer of marriage. The letter in effect insisted that he declare himself: did he still feel the same way about Henriette? Lamartine frets over it for a few days and then writes back, claiming that he cannot marry without his parents' consent, thus setting Henriette free. All this is somewhat disingenuous, of course; before being shuttled off to Italy, he had seemed quite willing to go against his parents' wishes and marry Henriette.*]

I learned a few days later that she would marry a new suitor. I regretted it, but in the end I understood that her parents were right not to sacrifice the future of this amiable child to the illusions of a seventeen-year-old. And so it came to an end, that dream that had been such a delightful but short imaginary happiness.

I did not see her again for thirty years—not without regret, but without bitterness. There are certain apparitions that seem destined only to set a young man dreaming. Mademoiselle P*** was one such chimera. She was happy, and she deserved better than me. I was still a child; but I was sincere and loyal.

VII

After having spent several days staying in the hotel with Virieu, I went to room with Monsieur de la Chavanne. It was an easy walk. I only left Virieu at night, for the pleasure of seeing him again in the mornings. We were always together, except overnight.

When I arrived, Monsieur de la Chavanne was not at home; I was met instead by the old Neapolitan cook and by the ravishing girl Graziella. She opened up the little room that had been assigned to me; she unpacked my bag and put it away in the armoire; then she knelt down and set to work on getting the wrinkles out of my clothes. With every pose, I discovered some new grace and charm in her body. But she did seem a little too timid, and she was paler than she had appeared the first time I had seen her, at the table. I hardly dared raise my eyes to her; we exchanged at most a few insignificant words. I imagined that she was simply one of my sisters who was welcoming me home after a long journey. The simplicity of her clothes removed all profane thoughts from my mind.

VIII

After I was settled in my room, we went to the dining room, where she went back to her work. Antoniella came back from the floor she had been on before my arrival, overseeing the girls who were rolling cigarettes. Dinner was served; Antoniella and Graziella sat at the table as on the first day.

"This one," Monsieur de la Chavanne told me in a bantering tone, "is called Antoniella. She's a good girl, and she does essential work for me here. She's the one who chooses, hires, or fires the novices for my little convent, who number several hundred, and who work with the tobacco and make the cigars; she knows the families of the *lazzaroni* and the poor people who have too many children and who ask to have them come work at the factory. She handles her work marvelously; she lives and eats with me in order to get my orders and transmit them to the others. Everyone likes her, both overseers and workers; all these little working girls are like her children, or her sisters.

She's the one who tells the families about any complaints regarding the little ones, and she helps me keep things from slipping into total disorder. In Naples, they call her the mother of the *sigarette* girls." At these words, Antoniella burst out laughing. Monsieur de la Chavanne looked at her out of the corner of his eye and smiled too.

"Now this little one, still basically a child, is being taught French by Antoniella so that one day she will serve as an interpreter between the management and the directors, our compatriots; she's called Graziella. She's the daughter of a poor fishing family on Procida, one with too many children. I pay her what I pay a cigar worker, and she gives the money to her family at the end of the month. But she doesn't work with the others, and she eats with us in order to stick close to Antoniella, her friend and protector. She helps her around the place, and she passes on my orders to the *servilia*—that is, the Neapolitan domestics. She's still quite a child, but a good one, and everybody likes her; I act more like a father to her than a boss. Don't worry about her; she's in charge of everything around here; she's my second-in-command, or rather, my second-in-giving-commands. If you want anything, let her know; she is at your service; but you really have to see her costume, which is that of a young Procidan, a peasant of the islands from which Naples gets its most beautiful, most charming, hardest-working women. Their costume is considered servile in Naples but noble on their island. Go," he said to Graziella, "and dress like a Procidan. Antoniella can help you."

The beautiful girl went out with Antoniella and, a few minutes later, returned in a totally different set of clothes. It was like one of those changes in decor that alters the whole scene. On her feet, Graziella wore a sort of Oriental slipper of yellow goatskin that left the heels exposed, while the leather was embroidered with red straps sprinkled with silver sequins. Her stockings were blue and thick, not of mesh but of a kind of heavy felt; a brown woolen skirt with big pleats tumbled down over her feet; a low-necked top of green cloth came down below her waist, leaving her bust buttoned up tight, but the buttons would allow a young mother to readily open it and nurse her children; the sleeves were decorated with stripes and rich embroidery, worn by rich and poor alike. Her coiffure was simply a matter of having her hair wrapped up atop her head like a kind of turban; her throat and ears were adorned with necklaces and pendants in the Greek style, large and thin, which tinkled like the bells on a horse when she moved her torso. Graziella's blush, as she displayed herself thus, was born of both modesty and shame—modesty at sensing herself being admired, and shame at feeling beautiful. We all sat there mute, and if she had not been almost a child, we would have lowered our eyes as well.

Soon she went off and quickly returned wearing her normal daily clothes. But the deed was done: the marvelous figure had been endowed with its special accent; I could not forget what I had seen, and when I looked at her in her daily clothes, she seemed only a pale image of herself. This outfit consisted of an ordinary dress, of rough cloth, brown, closed up practically to the chin, with neither stripes nor embroidery, and with a blue scarf tied around the neck; her feet were almost bare in black, worn-down slippers.

Such was the caterpillar. But the butterfly—?

IX

Virieu came to see me one day. His father, during the siege of Lyon, had been the general in charge of the Lyonnais cavalry. Monsieur de la Chavanne had been among those who followed him out in his final sortie and had almost been witness to his death. The two of them talked about that somber day at length. Virieu dined with us and was just as struck as I had been with the Greek beauty of the young Procidan.

That evening, Virieu and I went out, and I escorted my friend back to his hotel.

As we passed by the end of the Rue de Tolède, we went into the Florentin, across from the theater, out of curiosity. This was the public gaming house, legal and overseen by the police. Huge tables, surrounded by silent gamblers, filled the rooms; on the green felt of the tables were piles of silver and gold before each player. It did not take long for us to be tempted; we played for a few écus and lost. We returned the next day, and the day after that, and we continued to lose. This went on for several days. We couldn't understand why chance kept going against us. At one point we were seated by a window complaining when an elderly Neapolitan man came up to us and told us that as long as we continued playing like that, with no plan, the outcome would always be the same; gaming, he explained, was not a matter of chance but, rather, a science, a science from which one ought not expect more than what it is capable of giving, but only a modest, limited set of winnings; he said that he himself had in the past been a victim, but that today he made his living from the very thing that had once ruined him. We listened to him in astonishment; he perceived this, and lowering his voice further he proposed giving us lessons in gaming, having been, he said, a croupier, and therefore being in possession of *masses* of cards with which he would prove his theory. We accepted with that docile ignorance of youth, and we arranged to meet him the next day at Virieu's hotel, on the Rue des Florentins. The old man came that next evening, and having laid out on the table what is called a *masse*, that is, a quantity of ten or twelve hands of cards, the proof commenced.

"Play any way you wish," he said to us. "I will bet that by the end of the evening you will lose, and I will win." He dealt the cards, we played, and we lost; he didn't win a lot, but he won something every time. We went through the proof some twenty times, always with the same odds; we were confounded.

"So why aren't you rich?" we asked him.

"Because riches are not the result of good luck," he replied, "but of hard work. I did not promise that you would learn how to make millions, but how to win some money. Shall we continue?"

"Yes."

"Well, then! Now I'm going to explain my system to you and teach you its basis; follow me closely. What is the game, *Trente et quarante*? A game in which the player, playing against the house, which always bets, wins every time the color *rouge* or *noir*—upon which he bets liberally—wins by coming as close as possible to forty without going over; for when you go over, you've lost. Therefore, it's a matter of the player conjecturing carefully which is the color, the red or the black, that represents the highest probability or getting the winning number, and conforming his play to that."

X

The croupier, relying on experience and his system, continued playing for an hour and, fitting his bets to his conjectures, indeed gained modest sums, while we, playing on mere chance, always kept on losing. At this point he left, promising to return the next day. It remained to be seen if longer experience would confirm this art of almost always winning a modest amount. The next day, and for the twenty days after that, we became convinced: the croupier spoke the truth: he would gain a few écus while we would lose napoléons. We became serious and intent about it: "But what is the cause? Because after all, chance is only an effect whose cause is unknown; let us continue and seek to find the cause."

The croupier came around for the rest of the winter, and we devoted whole evenings to him, sometimes at the hotel and sometimes at the house of Monsieur de la Chavanne; we did nothing but play cards, and we played no game but *Trente et quarante*. The French friends of Monsieur de la Chavanne would converse, standing around the brazier where olive wood burned soundlessly, giving off warmth without flame. Antoniella and Graziella would be doing some women's work on the sofa. From time to time Graziella would look in my direction and force a smile, but then she would immediately revert to her serious expression; she seemed to be saying, "What a pity that such a smart young man should be so stupid about cards!" The croupier always came out ahead, and the only thing we learned was in watching him pocket a few *carlini* at the end of the evening.[5]

XI

And that is how we spent that winter in Naples, before an early spring came and began to gleam up on the ice and mountains of Castellammare. We could hear Vesuvius grumbling and see it shooting out puffs of smoke like the foam on great waves of fire. Virieu did not feel well and began staying in. One day as I was descending the staircase in his hotel, I bumped into Monsieur de Humboldt, the diplomat.[6] He embraced me like a father. He proposed to take me with him on a trip to Calabria to study the volcano when the eruption, the signs of which had only just begun, was at its fiercest. I accepted with delight, though I also felt a little sad when I looked at Graziella and thought about her. But at that point, we had not yet come to an understanding.

Book V

I

Monsieur de Humboldt came to pick me up. When I got up in his carriage and he asked me who that pretty girl was, I looked over at her, and I could see tears in her eyes. Why was she crying? Why did she follow our carriage with her eyes?

The horses took us along the Pompeii road and toward Torre dell'Annunziata, a little village before Castellammare, built up on one of the great roots of the mountain. We took rooms in an inn even closer to Vesuvius, and we sent out to find guides and mules to take us up to the hermit's dwelling; his cell had been built up on the summit of the habitable cone. After a wearying walk of two or three hours, sometimes on hardened, slippery lava, sometimes on still warm cinders that the wind swirled around us, blinding us, we stopped on the last somewhat flat spot on the mountain. Turning around, we seemed to be swimming in the sky itself: the sea, the islands, the capes, Naples, all of it grew out of the earth far below us. We cried out in wonder. The hermit's dwelling was there; the hermit himself was no longer spending the night there, fearing to be surprised in his sleep by an outburst of subterranean lightning. We sat down on the bench by the door, contemplating the marvels at our feet, as they seemed to float in the air below. Eventually the hermit arrived on his donkey. The donkey was loaded with casks of Lacryma

Christi wine. The hermit kept such provisions there for his guests, and he charged them well for it. But apart from that, he was a good old fellow who belonged to no order of monks in Naples but, rather, to that fictive nomadic order that attaches itself to some site with natural phenomena that attracts the tourist and makes a living out of it. This one? He was of the Order of Vesuvius. He changed his cell when the mountain gave warning signs that a catastrophe was imminent. The rest of the time, he provided drinks for the curious visitors—a café both picturesque and holy.

Monsieur de Humboldt and I took our places at his table, conversing with the monk about the ways of the mountain, its preludes and its eruptions. I determined to get as deep down in the crater as I could to study it. There was no real use in all this for me, being neither a scholar nor a naturalist; I scarcely even knew the names of the scientific samples I proposed bringing back with me, but I was at that age where a man wants to test his courage, no matter what it costs, and I was evidently of the race of Empedocles, who left his sandals behind on the edge of Etna. I had two of the guides return to Torre dell'Annunziata to find the ropes that would hold me as I descended into the deep crater. Monsieur de Humboldt teased me about all my preparations and did his best to argue me out of the pointless scheme; but I was proud of my bravery, and I woke up more firmly determined on my adventure than ever.

II

Vesuvius had been quiet during the night. The sunrise was dazzling; the only thing you could see was the yellowish smoke heaving, at intervals, out of the sharp cone, up above our heads.

We followed our guides using the ropes they had

brought up the night before. We were climbing now, not walking anymore. Any number of times we were able to hear burning rock falling onto the moving bed of ashes, causing little whirlwinds of dust to blow up around us and blot out the light of day for a moment; it was as if the inhabitants of this infernal region were angry at the approach of living people. We threw ourselves down on the ground to avoid rebounding projectiles; we would wait, and when the rocks ceased rolling, our spirits would recover.

Finally, we arrived at the extreme border of the volcano, and we sat down to gaze and take the measure of that terrifying abyss, half-luminous and half-shadowy, that hollowed out endlessly below our feet. It was like an enormous funnel whose depths and rims showed the five or six different colorings left by the recent eruptions. Here, a region of white salt imitated a new snowfall; there, strips of yellow sulfur looked like gold poured out of a crucible; farther off, rocks were cracked and smoking, held in place on the edge under their own weight; elsewhere, stalactites cooled in place;[7] elsewhere again, fields of a brownish substance whose name I did not know; and finally, toward the middle of the depths of the crater, clouds of smoke thrusting and twisting, as if the abyss were exhaling them or extinguishing them; enormous rocks were lifted from the beds by the power of interior flames, which, however, did not have enough strength to push them farther; and everywhere you could hear the rustling sound of flames, as if mountain lakes had been set on fire, tracing out their geographic edges in a world composed of fire. Everything was marvel; everything was terror.

My guides were nearby with their ropes, and they said, "This is enough to make you turn back, I think; what more would you expect to see if you went down there?"

"I want to have touched it," I replied. Getting up

from the pile of hot sand where I was sitting, I passed my arms through the ropes and started a slow descent down the inner edge of the funnel. None of the guides would agree to come down with me, but they all worked hard to support and direct me from above, from the rocks on the ledge. After some minutes I came to the very bottom of the abyss; but the heat was increasing as the walls of the funnel narrowed, and my shoes were getting so hot that they burned my feet; only enough shoe remained to protect my skin. I cooled them in the spots where the ground was not molten and retained a little of the coolness of earth. I vaulted over streams of fire that I could hear boiling between their banks and then ran to get to the less fiery crust, where I rested. I would have been lost if the wind had suddenly changed and blown the flames and smoke back in my direction, instead of swirling toward the opposite rock face. They called to me from above. I stayed on, though, making a little haul of minerals that I knotted up in my kerchief to take back up to daylight with me. At last, after two or three hours of this perilous promenade, down in hell in the middle of the day, I signaled to the guides to begin pulling me up. I went up the way I had come down, with no damage except to my scorched shoes and clothing. A shout of victory and happiness went up when my feet hit the ground; Monsieur de Humboldt congratulated me and explained the objects I had brought back with me from the abyss. We returned to the hermit's cell to find him shocked by my daring, and a frugal dinner there, accompanied by Lacryma Christi, helped us all forget my folly.

That evening, I would have given my life to undo that ridiculous adventure. If I had been tempted by the desire to force Nature to divulge her secrets, the whole thing would have been sublime; but tempted by mere ignorance, my boldness was only laughable. Vanity deserves nothing more. I had been vain—that was all. I deserved nothing but contempt.

III–IV–V

[*Lamartine and von Humboldt stay on while the volcano erupts, causing considerable damage and misery to some local inhabitants. Lamartine gets as close to the molten lava as he dares, putting the tip of a cane in and watching it burn; when the lava seems to be changing course, they flee. Later, von Humboldt returns to Naples, and Lamartine proceeds to Castellammare. Lamartine sees Sorrento from afar, and it makes him think of Tasso, a moment described in an early sequence in* Graziella. *Here, he adds: "Tasso arrived disguised as a peasant from Abruzzo, at the home of his sister, who was married to a gentleman farmer from Sorrento. And it was there that he was recognized, and his rustic clothes removed and replaced by those suited to a poet and a knight, and it was there that he completely regained his reason after some months of rest. I visited the site of this Homeric scene, worthy of* The Odyssey.*"]*

VI

After several days of traveling through that beautiful region, I rented a small boat and went to visit the mysterious temple of Paestum and Cava di Terrini, the most beautiful locale on the coast. Then after two weeks spent in these solitary excursions, when I thought that communications would have been reestablished between Torre dell'Annunziata and Naples, by means of earth and ashes heaped up over the bed of lava, I returned to my inn at Vesuvius, now a drowsy place again, and I took a carriage to Naples. My heart and my thoughts were always centered on Graziella; everything that I would not say I felt all the more, and I believed it would all be evident to that ravishing child.

As I mounted the stairs at San Pietro Martyr, I was surprised not to hear Graziella's voice calling out from the gallery. Everything was quiet and still in the old monastery. Monsieur de la Chavanne was with the factory's board of directors, and Antoniella was at work overseeing the cigar makers; my room had been locked. The cook, seeing my surprise, said, "Oh, you won't be seeing the little lady around anymore; she left for the island, to be with her family. We haven't heard anything from her, but we think she went to her grandmother's house on Ischia, where she'll stay until the fall. Here's a letter she insisted I give you as soon as you returned; take it and read!"

It was written or, rather, scrawled in Neapolitan: "*Gia che sei partito non posser piu restar. Non ti revedro mai: La Damizella.*" That is, "I haven't been able to rest since you left; I don't see you anymore." One or two teardrops had left their trace on the thick yellow paper.

The letter clarified what her gaze had been unable to make me understand. I went to my room and threw myself on the bed and began to weep. Virieu arrived a few moments later to see if there had been any news of me. He asked why I was crying, and I showed him the letter.

"Well, look at this! It's like the start of a novel! You'll have to develop the plot carefully though, or I'll get bored."

"Don't joke," I said. "Tears are serious when a girl is fourteen."

I waited until Antoniella came back, and I asked if she knew where her young friend was. "No," she said, "but I went to ask her father, on the docks at Pausilippo. There was nobody there; the neighbors told me they hadn't seen her and that she was probably with her family on Procida, at her grandmother's. After you went on your trip with the German scholar, she stopped confiding in me, and she wept a great deal."

VII

I waited until Monsieur de la Chavanne returned from the board meeting. "Ah," he exclaimed when he saw me, "it would seem that you have been the cause of Graziella's despair and flight. We haven't been able to find her in Naples, and we think that she fled to escape her unhappiness, which was too much for her, and probably went to her grandmother's on Procida. Her good sense will eventually bring her back, you can be sure of that, and if you want to see her, she'll probably be back before autumn."

I wanted to see her sooner than that. I knew where to find her, and I knew that she had quit her job with Monsieur de la Chavanne out of grief at my departure with Monsieur de Humboldt. I knew that she loved me and that her flight was really a wild declaration of that love. I was heartsick; I could not endure being far away from her. I narrated, in another book, how it was that I rejoined her at Procida. The details that I am about to divulge are the only difference between the fiction of the novel and the truth of the book. My youthful vanity could not allow me to admit that my first love was for a cigarette maker rather than a coral worker, which in fact she did become later. Is there anything vanity will not color?

And now, having admitted it today, I can say that the rest of the novel is completely correct. She was just as young, as naive, as pure, as religious as I represented her in the novel. All the scenes are true. The scenes and the actors are just as they were. The work was less vulgar, and that is all. Thus, our trip to Procida's port to buy a new boat and make a gift of it to the family, the joy of the grandmother in receiving it, the children's exclamations of delight—all of this is narrated, not invented. The same is true of our life on the island and our feelings: the night on the terrace, where we set up a tent, the day among the vines, where we lived the happy and simple lives of the *lazzaroni*.[8]

VIII

Toward the end of May, my family sent Virieu a letter to make me come home and leave behind the suspect life they imagined I was living at Margellina. Monsieur de la Chavanne had no doubt told my mother about it.[9] Virieu, out of friendship for me, hurried to Naples and pulled me away with him unexpectedly. I left Graziella in a faint, in tears. I decided I would return to live and die on Procida. In Milan, I stayed on after Virieu had gone; I was determined to try out the *Trente et quarante* system that I had so conscientiously studied with the old croupier the previous winter in Naples. I promised Virieu I would not stay on long but would return to my family within two weeks.

Milan had a casino open daily at the La Scala theater. That was the place I chose for my experiment. I tried to apply the old croupier's theory. I thought that without reaching the number of forty, there was more chance with many small-numbered cards than with five or six high numbers. On the other hand, experience had taught me that the high numbers and the low ones were dealt in series and not alternatively. I concluded that one could, by attentively observing the cards dealt, infer the ones that were about to come and thereby end up winning. I followed this system rigorously, and in fact I did win every evening.

I stayed in Milan for two weeks and then left for Lyon with a Swiss businessman from Lausanne and his servant, who showed me great hospitality both on the road and in their home for several days. The old Swiss was a liberal and no friend to the emperor, Napoleon. I shared his sentiments, following the tradition of my family. The inscriptions that I read on the stone boundary markers—

Liberty, Equality, Fraternity—made me tremble with sympathy.

After several days resting in Lausanne, I took a carriage and returned to Mâcon. My father was awaiting me and welcomed me as a father should, making no mention of my stupid foibles. I was home, and I was forgiven. What a fine father he was! I was sad, but I did not explain why. My mother wept with joy; my family hid their annoyance; but now everything was forgotten—except within my heart and within the ailing heart of Graziella. Alas, it was not long before I learned of her death and received her farewell letter, given to me by a traveler passing through Mâcon. Her last thoughts had been of me.[10]

TRANSLATOR'S NOTES

Translator's Introduction

1. Flaubert expresses his criticism of *Graziella* in a letter to Louise Colet, April 24, 1852, when he was in the midst of the long composition of *Madame Bovary*. Not surprisingly, given the task he was immersed in, he faults *Graziella* for its lack of realism, for the questionable credibility of its characters, and for what he sees as a number of missed opportunities in the execution of the story. He seems particularly unable to credit the chastity of the love between Graziella and Lamartine: "Et d'abord, pour parler clair, la baise-t-il, ou ne la baise-t-il pas?" See Jean Bruneau, ed., *Flaubert: Correspondance II* (Paris: Gallimard, Bibliothèque de la Pléiade, 1980), 77–79.

2. Roger Pearson, *Unacknowledged Legislators: The Poet as Lawgiver in Post-Revolutionary France* (Oxford: Oxford University Press, 2016), 324.

3. Michel Winock provides a comparison of the three works in *Les Voix de la liberté: Les écrivains engagés au dix-neuvième siècle* (Paris: Éditions du Seuil, 2001), 349–65.

4. William Fortescue, *Alphonse de Lamartine: A Political Biography* (New York: St. Martin's, 1983), 128. Fortescue's carefully researched study remains the best guide to the subject in English.

5. Richard Sennett, *The Fall of Public Man: On the Social Psychology of Capitalism* (New York: Vintage, 1976), 228.

6. Maurice Toesca, *Lamartine, ou l'amour de la vie* (Paris: Albin Michel, 1983), 465.

7. Sennett, *Fall of Public Man*, 231.

8. *Confidential Disclosures* was translated by Eugène Plunkett for Appleton & Co., in New York. The urgency of getting it into print in English was such that Plunkett apologized to the reader for his

translation of the poem "Le Premier regret." Plunkett says he hopes some future translator will do a better job, "having more leisure than we were allowed by the hurried publication of this translation, to do justice to the piece. . . ." Lamartine, *Confidential Disclosures*, trans. Eugène Plunkett (New York: Appleton, 1849), 283.

9. The four poems were "Á Elvire," "L'Immortalité," "Le Temple," and "Hymne au soleil."

10. Deborah Jenson, *Trauma and Its Representations: The Social Life of Mimesis in Post-Revolutionary France* (Baltimore: Johns Hopkins University Press, 2003), 156.

11. Elisabeth Bronfen, *Over Her Dead Body: Death, Femininity, and the Aesthetic* (New York: Routledge, 1992), 5.

12. Ibid., 13.

13. See Paul Viallaneix, "La Fable d'Elvire," *Romantisme* 3 (1971): 33–42. Viallaneix notes that many later writers adopted the tropes, including Musset, Vigny, and Nerval.

14. Julie Charles letter, in René Doumic, ed., *Lettres d'Elvire à Lamartine* (Paris: Hachette, 1905), 29.

15. Toesca, *Lamartine*, 139.

16. In the 1849 commentary on the poem "À Elvire," Lamartine wrote: "This was a love poem addressed to the memory of a young Neapolitan girl, the death of whom I narrated in *Confidences*. Her name was Graziella." Quoted in *Lamartine: Méditations*, ed. Fernand Letessier (Paris: Garnier, 1968), 330–31.

17. The sequence of romantic/sexual relationships is longer than this list suggests. Another important one took place very soon after Lamartine returned from Italy, in the summer of 1812, when he drifted into an affair with Nina de Pierreclau, married to a friend of his. The marriage was a relatively open one, and Nina bore Lamartine a son in March of the following year. Lamartine's sympathetic modern biographer Maurice Toesca excuses the poet's so quickly abandoning his fidelity to the Neapolitan girl by arguing that this affair was a "normal consolation or at least a convenient emotional outlet" after having to leave his young lover behind (Toesca, *Lamartine*, 98).

18. Valentine, the daughter of Lamartine's sister Cécile, lived from 1821 to 1894, and was her uncle's constant companion and mainstay in the last, increasingly troubled decades of his life. There

has long been speculation that the two may have been lovers, and that they may have secretly married. In any case, he came to depend on her entirely as the family slipped into poverty during the 1860s and his mental powers began to wane.

19. Jean des Cognets, *La Vie intérieure de Lamartine* (1934), quoted in Abel Verdier, *Les Amours italiennes de Lamartine* (Paris: La Colombe, 1963), 44–45.

20. Lamartine, *"Graziella" et "Raphaël,"* ed. Jean des Cognets (Paris: Garnier, 1960), 239. The theme of ordinary language as inadequate to the poet's needs is a frequent one in Lamartine's poetry; see the discussion in Pearson, *Unacknowledged Legislators*, 334–43.

21. The 1844 negotiations and payments for these and other works are detailed in Toesca, *Lamartine*, 392–93.

22. Lamartine's negotiations and relationships with publishers, as well as his attitudes toward the world of print, are studied in Nicolas Courtinat, "Formes et usages de l'imprimé chez Lamartine, 1830–1849," *Revue d'Histoire littéraire de la France* 108, no. 2 (April–June 2008): 327–45.

23. Eugène Pelletan (1813–1884), a writer and politician, was associated with Lamartine in the great years of the 1840s and was himself elected to the Chambre des Députés in the 1860s.

24. On a number of complications in this story, including the publisher's sudden inability to fulfill his contract, see Toesca, *Lamartine*, 396–99.

25. Fortescue, *Alphonse de Lamartine: A Political Biography*, 16–17.

26. Lamartine's *Mémoires inédits, 1790–1815* was posthumously published in 1870 (Paris: Louis de Ronchaud, 1870).

27. Lamartine actually wrote the novel in 1844 and published it in 1849. The phrasing he uses is significant—"the true novel [*roman vrai*], *Graziella*."

28. Louis Nicolas Philippe Auguste, Comte de Forbin (1779–1841), was a painter and later director of the Musée du Louvre.

29. Verdier quotes from a letter of January 26, 1813, referring to "M. Dareste et son Antoniella"—that is, Monsieur Dareste and *his* Antoniella. Quoted in Verdier, *Les Amours italiennes de Lamartine*, 64.

30. Letter of April 2, 1819, quoted in ibid., 64.

31. Letter of December 16, 1816, quoted in ibid., 74.

32. Jenson, *Trauma and Its Representations*, 157.

33. In his commentary on the 1849 republication of *Méditations*, Lamartine offers a different narrative about how he became a poet, listening as a child to his father reading aloud from Voltaire's *Mérope*. It is a narrative about the birth of imagination and the beginnings of a sense of the power and capabilities of words. But in 1856, in the first of his sequence of essays titled *Cours familier de littérature*, he gave a different story, this time about listening as a child to his mother reading aloud from a religious book, "un volume de dévotion." Pearson discusses both, noting that the maternal presence in the latter creates "a world of murmured communion in which . . . communication and reception fuse in an inaudible dialogue permitting access to a mysterious and wordless beyond" (*Unacknowledged Legislators*, 377).

34. Thomas G. Pavel, *The Lives of the Novel: A History* (Princeton, N.J.: Princeton University Press, 2013), 184. This is Pavel's own translation of a book he originally wrote in French, *La Pensée du roman* (Paris: Gallimard, 2003).

35. Letter of May 21, 1812, quoted in Toesca, *Lamartine*, 96–97.

36. A good discussion of Lamartine's ideas regarding the literature of the people is in Jenson, *Trauma and Its Representations*, especially 166–82. Fortescue sees the enterprise in a more sardonic way, concluding that Lamartine's worker novels failed because "his workers were too obviously idealized portraits, his preaching of Christian moral virtues was too crude, and his settings were too far removed from the factories and urban squalor which increasingly featured in French working class life" (Fortescue, *Alphonse de Lamartine*, 256). Even sourer were the reactions of contemporaries like Barbey d'Aurevilly and Flaubert; the latter called the preface to *Geneviève* "madness taken to the point of idiocy" (quoted in Toesca, *Lamartine*, 482).

37. Henry Louis Gates Jr., *The Signifying Monkey: A Theory of Afro-American Literary Criticism* (New York: Oxford University Press, 1988), 152–58.

38. Marius-François Guyard, "Lamartine et *Paul et Virginie*," *Revue d'Histoire littéraire de la France* 89, no. 5 (September–October 1989): 891–99.

39. Jillian Heydt-Stevenson, "'Amber Does Not Shed So Sweet a Perfume as the Veriest Trifles Touched by Those We Love': Engaging with Community through Things in Bernardin de Saint-Pierre's *Paul et Virginie* and Alphonse de Lamartine's *Graziella*," *Engaged Romanticism: Romanticism as Praxis*, ed. Mark Lussier and Bruce Mastsunaga (Cambridge, U.K.: Cambridge Scholars, 2008), 36–37.

40. The widow of Bernardin de Saint-Pierre, now Madame Aimé Martin, had become a family friend; she and her husband, a well-connected professor, helped get Lamartine elected to the Académie Française in 1830. See Toesca, *Lamartine*, 271–72.

41. Jean-Marie Gleize, in *Poésie et Figuration* (Paris: Seuil, 1983), 19–46, cites this incident as an example of Lamartine's near-mystical belief in the power of poetry to transcend the limits of ordinary language. A valuable discussion of what Aimée Boutin calls "the poetry of listening" is in her *Maternal Echoes: The Poetry of Marceline Desbordes-Valmore and Alphonse de Lamartine* (Newark: University of Delaware Press, 2001), 68–92.

42. Lamartine, *"Graziella" et "Raphaël,"* 239.

43. Pearson, *Unacknowledged Legislators*, 385.

44. On Lamartine's self-presentation in the novel as artist, see Laurent Darbellay, *"Graziella*: portrait(s) du jeune homme en artiste," in *Lamartine: autobiographie, mémoires, fiction de soi*, ed. Nicolas Courtinat (Clermont-Ferrand: Presses Universitaires Blaise Pascal, 2009), 129–43.

45. Verdier, *Les Amours italiennes de Lamartine*, 44. The other figures given are of interest too: another 13,500 copies of *Confidences* were sold, and 53,000 of *Raphaël*, against only 39,000 for the great volume of poems that made him a famous writer, *Méditations*.

46. Émile Henriot used the phrase "bréviares du coeur" in his preface to Eugène Fromentin's 1863 novel *Dominique* (Paris: Garnier, 1936).

Chapter 1

1. The relative was Madame Eugénie La Haste, a pretty and flirtatious young married woman from Lyon, cousin to Lamartine's

mother; Lamartine met her in a previous stay in Lyon in 1809. The group set off for Italy on July 1, 1811. Lamartine was twenty-one at the time, not eighteen. The vague phrase about "the soul's early passions" is a way of glossing over the fact that Lamartine's parents wanted to get him away from his romantic attachment to Henriette Pommier, the daughter of a local justice of the peace. The trip would also serve the purpose of keeping Lamartine out of the clutches of Napoleon's recruiters. For the many differences between the tale as told here and what seems to have really happened, see the Translator's Introduction.

2. When Lamartine was seven, the family moved to their estate in Milly, in the Burgundy region of east-central France. His happiest memories were of his youth in Milly, and when much later in life financial troubles forced him to consider selling the place, the idea was agony to him. The village today is renamed Milly–Lamartine.

3. Madame de Staël's novel *Corinne* (1807) was, like Goethe's *Werther*, an enormously popular and influential tale of doomed love. Corinne is a poet with a passionate, romantic nature, residing in Rome. The novel helped fix Italy in the French public mind as an exotic locale.

4. The line comes from Goethe's poem "Kennst du das Land," which is sung by the character Mignon in the novel *Wilhelm Meisters Lehrjahre* (1795–96), though the reference there is to lemon trees not myrtles. The same line is adapted in a poem in de Staël's *Corinne*, where it is changed to orange trees.

5. The father was the famous and accomplished tenor Giacomo Davide (he dropped the final *e* on his name after a concert tour in England). He had a son, Giovanni, born in 1790, who by 1811 was already a well-known and accomplished tenor; what follows, however, reveals that the young person traveling with Davide was not Giovanni.

6. In his *Mémoires inédits*, Lamartine identifies the old painter as Giunto Tardi (Book III, chapter xvii). This was evidently Filippo Giuntotardi (1768–1831).

7. The painter's brother was Pietro Giuntotardi. He is also mentioned in the journals of Claire Clairmont, where his name is spelled with a hyphen, Giunto-tardi. *The Journals of Claire Clare-*

mont, ed. Marion Kingston Stocking (Cambridge, Mass.: Harvard University Press, 1968), 143. In Mariana Starke's popular guidebook *Information and Directions for Travelers on the Continent* (London: John Murray, 1828), we read that "the most eminent Professor of Languages at Rome is Sig. Giuntotardi. . . . Sig. Giuntotardi's fee is one zecchino for three lessons" (499). A brief biography can be found in Letitzia Norci Cagiano de Azevedo, *Lo Specchio del Viaggiatore: Scenari italiani tra Barocco e Romanticismo* (Rome: Edizioni de storia e letteratura, 1992), 165ff.

8. Cola di Rienzo (c. 1313–54) rose from humble origins to become Tribune of Rome; he was also associated with an ill-fated attempt to unify Italy. He was considered a hero by many, including Petrarch.

9. In 1798, the revolutionary French government under Napoleon, known at this time as the Directorate, proclaimed Rome as a republic; General Mack, an Austrian soldier, was put in charge of the Neapolitan army by the Emperor Francis II, with the charge of putting down the infant republic. His triumph was short-lived, and he became a prisoner of war under Napoleon. After escaping, he led the Austrian army against Napoleon, but he ultimately surrendered at the battle of Ulm in 1805.

10. Vincenzo Monti (1754–1828) was an Italian poet and patriot whom Lamartine saw as enthusiastically supporting the ideals of the French Revolution; others saw him as an opportunist, and indeed his allegiances did change significantly. There was nothing equivocal, however, about the patriotic reputation of Vittorio Alfieri (1749–1803), one of the greatest poets and playwrights of the era; like Lamartine, he was an anti-monarchist who was also an aristocrat, and like Lamartine, he cautioned against revolutionary excesses.

11. Lamartine's chronology is often inexact—or, rather, fictionalized. In fact he left Rome for Naples in the first week of April 1812.

12. Calabria refers to the southwestern region of Italy. France had taken Naples over in 1799, at first allowing Ferdinand to reign, but in 1808 Napoleon made his brother-in-law, Joachim Murat, King of Naples; he reigned until Napoleon's fall in 1815. At that time Ferdinand was restored to the throne.

13. Fra Diavolo was the name given to the guerrilla leader Michele Pezza (1771–1806). The name means "brother devil."

14. Aymon de Virieu (1788–1841) was the son of the Comte de Virieu and a member of the old aristocracy; the family can trace its history to the twelfth century. The two boys met at the Collège des Pères de la Foi at Belley, when Lamartine was thirteen and Virieu fifteen. Their friendship lasted until Virieu's early death; as Maurice Toesca put it, Virieu became "a sort of permanent confidante-confessor" (Toesca, *Lamartine*, 84). Again, the detail of the chronology in this passage is inexact: Virieu actually joined Lamartine in January 1812, and the two friends went to Naples together.

15. His mother's relative was Antoine Dareste de la Chavanne, director of the tobacco manufacturing facility in Naples. Lamartine gives a fuller description of him in *Mémoires inédites*: see the Appendix.

16. The castle was originally known as La Sirena and has a sinister reputation: it is said to be the place where Queen Joanna II of Naples had her lovers murdered; it was bought by Anna Carafa and restored and is now known as the Villa Donn'Anna.

17. The homeless and poor of Naples were traditionally known as *lazzaroni*, from the Hospital of St. Lazarus, which offered them some shelter. The word is often used, as Lamartine uses it here, to denote simply a class of idlers or street people, without necessarily suggesting destitution.

18. Latin-style, or lateen, sails are triangular.

19. When Lamartine refers to the *Orient*, he usually means the region we would call the Middle East today.

20. A minor inconsistency: Lamartine had earlier told us that the St. Francis statue was affixed to the stern of the boat.

21. The Baie des Trépassés, usually translated as the Bay of the Dead, is located on the west coast of Finistère, in Brittany, France. Legend tells of dead souls haunting the place. The allusion takes us out of Italy for a moment to a French scene with ominous overtones.

Chapter 2

1. Ugo Foscolo (1778–1827), Italian revolutionary and poet, published his novel *The Letters of Jacopo Ortis* in 1798. Foscolo had

hailed Napoleon's coming to power, believing he would liberate Italy, but when Napoleon signed a treaty giving Venice to the Austrians, Foscolo's disappointment gave rise to this impassioned novel. As Lamartine says, Foscolo writes in clear imitation of Goethe's *The Sorrows of Young Werther* (1778), but his hero is plagued more by political disappointment than unrequited love. And just as in *Werther*, the main character ends in suicide.

2. Jacques-Henri Bernardin de Saint-Pierre (1737–1814) published *Paul et Virginie* in 1787; like *Werther*, it was a book that took a generation by storm and remained popular well into the nineteenth century. It certainly had a major impact on Lamartine, and much in *Graziella* is inspired by it; see the introduction for more detail on some of the many relationships between these two important texts of "innocent love."

3. The *Annals* and the *Histories* of the ancient Roman Tacitus (AD 56–120) could be read by progressives as supportive of liberty and a republican mode of government, and his tales of Rome have a sweep and an intensity that clearly appealed to the young Lamartine. There is also an undercurrent of contrast between the grandeur of Rome in Tacitus's day and the debased state of Italy in the early nineteenth century. Ironically, another keen reader of Tacitus was the man Lamartine detested, Napoleon, who liked to have himself portrayed as a kind of new Caesar, recalling the modern age to the greatness of the past; Napoleon cited and admired the ancient Roman figures that Tacitus described frequently.

4. The *Dying Gaul*, sometimes called the *Dying Galatian* or the *Dying Gladiator*, resides in the Capitoline museum in Rome. It was already famous in Lamartine's day and widely reproduced and copied; Napoleon had taken the original to France and put it on display in the Louvre, but it was returned to Rome in 1816, after his fall.

5. *Paul et Virginie* is of course a novel, but calling it a poem suggests Lamartine's expansive, Romantic definition of poetry as something that evokes deep feeling, not simply something in meter and rhyme. See Roger Pearson, *Unacknowledged Legislators*, especially 380–86.

Chapter 4

1. In Tasso's 1581 epic poem "La Gerusalemme Liberata" (Jerusalem Delivered), Herminie or Erminia is one of the maidens of Antioch; she falls in love with the Christian knight Tancred. Leaving her own people, she hides in a forest at one point and is cared for by a humble family of shepherds, a sequence that is somewhat echoed by the situation in *Graziella*.

2. This is one of the passages that greatly exasperated Flaubert, who found all this chastity ringing false (see the Translator's Introduction). It may feel that way to a modern reader too, but in any case Lamartine's insistence on chastity goes well beyond what the nineteenth-century novel and its audiences demanded; it is clearly important to his overall design for the book. Vocabulary that hints at a suppressed sexuality is frequent, however; see, for example, the diction of section XXII.

3. Joachim-Napoléon Murat, brother-in-law to Napoleon, reigned as King of Naples from 1808 to 1815. Setting up establishments like schools and convents for his French compatriots suggests that a process like colonization was under way. When Napoleon fell, Murat fled to Corsica, where he was captured and soon after executed.

4. Lamartine seems to have forgotten that he had already introduced us to his friend Aymon de Virieu; there is no need to conceal his identity at this point.

5. The date is fictional. On the complications of dating the tale, see the Translator's Introduction.

6. The date of 1830 is apparently accurate; the biographer Maurice Toesca says the scene in the church took place in May 1830 (Toesca, *Lamartine, ou l'amour de la vie* [Paris: Albin Michel, 1969], 267). It was published as "Le Premier amour" in *La Mode* (June 12, 1830) and appeared as "Le Premier regret" in book form in the collection *Harmonies Poétiques et Religieuses*, which had its first publication on June 15, 1830.

7. Lake Nemi is about 135 miles north of Naples. The setting for the poem is therefore not quite that of *Graziella*. Another significant difference is that the beloved woman in the poem has a living mother.

Appendix

This excerpt is translated from *Mémoires inédits de Lamartine, 1790–1815* (Paris: Hachette, 1909).

1. Antoine Dareste de la Chavanne, 1760–1836.

2. Lamartine actually wrote the novel in 1844 and published it in 1849. The phrasing he uses is significant: "the true novel [*roman vrai*], *Graziella*."

3. Lamartine here subscribes to the nineteenth century's fascination with "physiognomy," the belief that certain facial features reveal certain character traits. The idea is almost universal with nineteenth-century novelists, from Balzac to Brontë.

4. The city of Lyon had rebelled against the new revolutionary government known as the Convention in August 1793, and troops were sent to encircle the city. After a two-month siege, the city capitulated, and the government announced that there would be massive punitive reprisals; some three hundred were killed in two days of mass executions. Monsieur de la Chavanne had fought on the side of the rebels and was living in Italy now in a kind of exile.

5. *Carlini* were metal-alloy coins that became obsolete after 1835.

6. This was the highly distinguished Wilhelm von Humboldt (1767–1835), who had been Prussian ambassador to Rome from 1802; he was also a philosopher and linguist, brother of the equally distinguished scientist Alexander von Humboldt.

7. Lamartine uses the word *stalactites*, but presumably these were stalagmites.

8. It is remarkable to observe Lamartine, at seventy-five years of age, continuing to insist on the truth of the narrative. Had he lived with the story so long that he had come to believe it?

9. Monsieur de la Chavanne probably did write such a letter, and with this very intention of getting Lamartine back home and out of Naples, but for very different reasons: see the Translator's Introduction.

10. Lamartine adds one paragraph more at the beginning of Book VI: "So that was my first love, both happy and unhappy, and my first stay in Italy. Since then, Italy has become my country [*patrie*], or at least, Italy has always remained for me the country of love."

Alphonse de Lamartine (1790–1869) was one of France's greatest Romantic writers. He was also a politician and one of the initiators of the revolution in France in 1848. He worked for the abolition of slavery, an end to capital punishment, and the establishment of universal education.

Raymond N. MacKenzie has translated many works of French literature, including Jules Barbey d'Aurevilly's *Diaboliques: Six Tales of Decadence* (Minnesota, 2015) and Stendhal's *Italian Chronicles* (Minnesota, 2017). He is professor of English at the University of St. Thomas in St. Paul, Minnesota.